Me Mam. Me Dad. Me.

'Touching and compelling to the end... It has sweetness and comedy, despite the gravity of its theme.'

***Sunday Times*, Book of the Week**

'It's hard to think of a work I've read for young people in recent times that has so much heart and humour, yet manages to explore such darkness... I heartily recommend this for all teens.'

***The Herald*, Books of the Year**

'An assured debut... Danny's honest distinctive voice brings humour and hope.'

The Bookseller

'For pitch-perfect teenage voices, you can't go wrong with Malcolm Duffy's *Me Mam. Me Dad. Me.*'

***Irish Times*, Books of the Year**

'The subject might be harrowing, but Duffy handles it with a light touch.'

Northern Echo

'Never once does the authenticity of the narration waver... The immediacy of the text is potent.'

Books For Keeps

'A powerful story of filial love when domestic violence gets in the way. An unforgettable central character and a truthful ending make for a truly impactful read.'

The Bookbag

Sofa Surfer

'Duffy confirms the promise of his *Me Mam. Me Dad. Me.* in a pertinent and empathetic novel.'

The Bookseller

'A story with a great heart, and wisdom, which shows the healing power of true friendship.'

Ele Fountain, author of *Melt*

'A crusading novel on a topic that sadly looks to be timeless.'

Financial Times

'This powerful and insightful story highlights the rise of homelessness while never losing humour or heart. It's about family, belonging and the importance of kindness and understanding. Great for book clubs and topical discussion in class.'

South Wales Evening Post

'Duffy's writing is touching, considerate, and illuminating... a fast-paced story with real heart that will leave all readers ever-changed. A must for all school libraries.'

The School Librarian

Fr peeopl wtih dylxeisa wrods dnt lwyas lkoo naorml. Dsyleicxs otefn mix up the sueneqce of leertts in a wrod. It cn mkae raednig a rael strggule. Tmmy hs kpet hs lraening diffcltuy hdedin. But nw hsa to cofrnnot hs graetst faer. Raedng in pbliuc.

READ BETWEEN THE LINES

MALCOLM DUFFY is a Geordie born and bred, but now he lives in Surrey with his wife and daughters. His debut, *Me Mam. Me Dad. Me.*, shortlisted for the Waterstones Children's Book Prize, also won the YA category of the Sheffield Children's Book Award 2019 and the Redbridge Children's Book Award 2019, as well as a host of other prizes. His second novel, *Sofa Surfer*, was shortlisted for the Redbridge Children's Book Award 2021, longlisted for the UKLA Book Awards 2021, nominated for the CILIP Carnegie Medal 2021 and selected for the Empathy Lab Read for Empathy Collection 2022.

Also by Malcolm Duffy

Me Mam. Me Dad. Me.

Sofa Surfer

READ BETWEEN THE LINES

Malcolm Duffy

ZEPHYR
An imprint of Head of Zeus

First published in the UK in 2022 by Zephyr, an imprint of Head of Zeus
This Zephyr paperback edition first published in the UK in 2023 by Head of Zeus,
part of Bloomsbury Publishing Plc

9 7 5 3 1 2 4 6 8

A catalogue record for this book is available from
the British Library.

ISBN (PB): 9781800241718
ISBN (E): 9781800241688

Typeset by Ed Pickford

Printed and bound in Great Britain by
CPI Group (UK) Ltd, Croydon CR0 4YY

Head of Zeus Ltd
5–8 Hardwick Street
London EC1R 4RG
WWW.HEADOFZEUS.COM

To Tallulah

'When truth is replaced by silence,
the silence is a lie.'

Yevgeny Yevtushenko

Contents

Nwe arrvail

I'm 45 per cent scared, 45 per cent excited. The other 10 per cent is confusion.

I wouldn't feel any of these things if he was just passing through. But he isn't. He's staying. Thanks to them. And their situation. Which is now our situation. Why did they have to go and do something so permanent? They didn't even bother asking me what I thought. Just went ahead and did it. My opinion, as usual, is worth less than an empty milk carton.

'Get a shuffle on,' shouts Dad.

I stand, staring into me open wardrobe. Not something I do very often. I normally decide on clothes in milliseconds. Sometimes even faster. But today I decide to choose carefully. Let him know what I'm like. Who he's dealing with. After much rummaging, I find the perfect thing.

'Ryan,' hollers Dad.

Once he gets above a certain level, I know it's time to move. A loud voice is usually as bad as it gets. Maybe a glare. Sometimes a stomp.

'What in God's name have you been doing up there?' he says, as I make me way downstairs.

'Gerrin' ready.'

He lets fly a huff.

She's waiting by the front door, looking anxious, fiddling with her cuff.

'We can't be late, Ryan,' she says, exasperated. 'Not today.'

Can't see how a few more minutes is gonna make much difference. Certainly not to him.

She sets the alarm, locks up and we climb into Dad's car. He starts the engine, and she puts a hand on his. Together they find first gear. They look at each other and smile, trying to reassure each other everything will be all right. Which it probably won't.

We move off.

Dad's car normally smells of damp socks and heat rub. Today it smells as though we've crashed into a cosmetics department. She's made an extra-large effort for the new arrival. Never seen her go to church, but if she did, imagine this is how she'd look: tweed jacket, long skirt, smart shoes, earrings, pearls, hair neat and tidy. Considering where we're going, it seems a total waste of time.

She is Dad's girlfriend. He's way too old to have one of those. The term should cease to apply after fifty. She's not a girl and is far more than a friend. The people who write dictionaries should work on that.

'Y'okay, sweet?' asks Dad.

That's new. Never heard him call Mam that. Called

her a few other words. The type that would get you in trouble. But that was mainly at the end.

'I'm fine, Mark,' she says, smiling at him.

Think he wants to smile back, but there's a busy junction coming up, and he's driving way faster than usual.

Can feel me insides being squeezed like a damp towel. Not sure what the knot's doing there. I'm not the one who's done anything wrong.

'Okay, Ryan?'

She asks me that a lot.

Always give her the same answer.

'Aye.'

Which is a lie so large it's borderline obese. I *was* okay, before this happened. Stare out of the window at the houses. Bet the people in them don't have a life like mine, where things have turned upside down. All they've got to worry about is what to have for dinner.

She glances nervously at her watch.

I've definitely made them late.

Feel a bit bad.

We're gettin' closer.

Can tell by the way her fidgeting has gone up a level.

Must be weird for her. But it's weird for me too.

I can see it up ahead.

The squat, brown building.

A shiver finds me spine.

Dad flicks his indicator. The car turns.

There in front of us.

HM Young Offenders Institution. Feltham.

Reelaesd

'See you soon, pal,' says the guy at the gate.

Not in the mood for jokes.

I grab my bag and walk outside.

I'm out. It's over. Finally, over.

I look around. Mum said she'd be here. Ten o' clock on the dot. Definitely said it. But I can't see her. Wouldn't blame her if she'd changed her mind, making me walk home instead. Not that she'd ever do that. Not my mum.

I walk up and down. Pacing's been my number-one hobby these last six months. A car drives fast into the car park, stops, brakes squealing, like they're here for a prison break. Doors open and slam shut. Three people get out. I spot her, hurrying towards me. Mum's not a runner, but she's trying her best. I sprint between the cars. As we get closer can see she's dressed smart. Don't know why she's made such an effort. It's only me.

The gap between us narrows. Her face becomes clearer. She's smiling. She's happy. So happy. Drop my bag and grab her. She seems smaller. Or have I got bigger?

'Tommy,' she sighs, holding me as close as she can. Mum's not the clingy type but then it's not every day your son comes out of prison. 'Sorry we're late. Traffic was bad.'

'No worries. You're here, Mum. That's all that matters.'

'My, there's some strength in those arms of yours,' she says, wiping her eyes, and stepping back to get a look at me.

'HM gyms. Best you can get. No queues. No membership fee.'

'Ya daft nutter.'

Mum punches me on the arm. Deserve to be punched in the face.

'You look good, Tommy.'

'Same as I did last month.'

She's been seeing me every week since I got put away.

'You look super nice too, Mum.'

She gazes up at me, as if I'm perfect.

'Mark and Ryan are here,' she says.

I glance over the cars and see Mark and his kid standing, looking awkward.

'Better not keep 'em waiting, eh?'

Pick up my bag and we walk towards them. Mum takes my hand. Can't remember when she last did that. Though she must have done once. When I was little. And innocent.

There are two new people in my life. First there's Mark, Mum's boyfriend. Met him a few times when he came with Mum to visit. He wasn't around before all this happened.

One day she came to visit and said she'd got a new man in her life. And then she dropped the bomb.

'Moving in with us. You sure, Mum?'

'Never been surer about anything, Tommy.'

The news shell-shocked me. Mum's the cautious type when it comes to guys. Been out with a few but no one's ever stayed. But when Mark arrived, she dived right in. After what I'd done, knew I couldn't argue. And he seems to make her happy. And it's her house.

Release Mum's hand.

'Hi, Mark.'

'Alreet, Tommy,' he says, in his deep Geordie voice. Gives me a firm handshake, the type you get from banging weights. He then gives me a full-on man-hug. What's that all about? I'm only his girlfriend's son.

Finally lets go.

Mark's a tall, slim, muscly guy. Could see why Mum fancied him. About the same height as me, hair cropped short, with a splash of grey above each ear. The big smile on his face says he's almost as happy as Mum to see me.

Housemate number two is standing further back, grinning at his shoes.

Ryan.

Bombshell number two was when Mum said Mark was bringing his son to live with us. Not like he's a pet rabbit or something. He's another human. Apart from my big mistake, nothing much ever happened to us. Then, all of a sudden, we've doubled the population of our house.

'He's a nice lad.'

'Sure he is. But he's not coming for tea. He's moving in.'

'We've got the room. It'll be fine.'

Not sure Ryan's gonna make the first move. So I do.

Approach the shoe-inspector. 'Tommy,' I say.

'Ryan,' says Ryan, lifting his head and smiling at me. I shake a hand that's as soft as uncooked liver. Ryan shakes mine. For a bit too long.

Prison's made me good at sizing people up. Ryan's a bookworm. No doubt. He's shorter than me, pale-faced, with glasses. Probably doesn't get out much. I can't imagine him making any school team. Apart from chess. Got long fingers too. Bet he plays the piano. Has a small scar on his forehead. Almost certainly not gang related.

'Ryan is a very bright, talented, hard-working young man,' says Mum, as if I'm none of those things. Apart from the young man bit.

Ryan nods as if he hears stuff like this every day.

'Aye.'

All four of us stand around, wondering what to say next.

'Thought we'd go for a pub lunch,' says Mum.

'Sound.'

We climb into Mark's car, a Lexus SUV. Better than Mum's old motor. I sit next to Ryan in the back. Mark starts the engine, and off we go. Take a final look over my shoulder at my old digs. Give them the finger.

'Seatbelt, Tommy,' says Mum, peering at me.

Hate being told what to do. Had way too much of that recently. But seeing as it's Mum doing the telling, I click my belt in place. I am so glad to be out. Press the button on my window and give my face a wind wash.

'Tommy, do you mind closing the window?' says Mark. 'It's making me ears go funny.'

I don't answer to him. I move the window up a fraction, stick my nose out, the way dogs do, and breathe in that sweet air.

'Please, Tommy,' sighs Mum.

I bring my nose in and the glass glides up.

Silence. Way too much silence. Made worse by the electric car. Guess it's hard to know what to say to someone like me. Not like I've come back from a month's holiday in Greece or a gap year in Asia. No photos of parties or me messing about on a beach. Just bad memories. The type you want to keep buried.

'What's up with your knee?'

Piano man.

'Nothing,' I say, clamping a hand on top to try to stop it dancing, which it likes to do at times like this.

'Was there tons of fighting in prison?'

'Ryan,' barks Mark.

'Only making conversation.'

'Well, make normal conversation.'

'It is normal. I saw a film once where these guys attacked each other with chair legs, and...'

'Ryan,' growls his dad. 'Sorry, Tommy. He's not normally like this.'

Wonder what normal Ryan's like.

'Do you play piano?' I ask.

Ryan nods.

One-nil to Tommy.

'Ryan's grade four.'

Wonder how Mum knows about grades. We haven't even got a piano.

'In fact, he's a good all-rounder,' says Mum.

Good for Ryan.

'Unlike me, eh? Even failed at crime.'

Ryan laughs.

'That's so not true, Tommy. You're brilliant at... art... drama... sport.'

Mum twists around to me and Ryan.

'All I want is for you two to get on.'

Yeah. Whatever.

Teh Inuch

I'm sitting dead close to a criminal.

Tommy's not what I imagined. Thought he'd be tougher, angrier, crazier. But he seems almost normal. I suppose even serial killers seem normal, until they start serially killing everyone.

We reach a pub, The Magpies.

Used to love gannin' to lunch with Mam and Dad. The three of us. This feels all wrong, like at school dinner when you find yourself on a table with kids from a different year. Kids who don't even want to be in the same postcode as you.

It takes eighty-four steps from the car to the pub.

'Table for Cavendish,' says Tommy's mam to a young waitress with multi-coloured hair.

Don't know why she bothered booking. There's no one here.

The rainbow-haired girl shows us to our table. I sit next to Tommy and grab a menu the size of a small door. They seem to have every consumable animal, vegetable and mineral on the planet. Tommy barely gives the menu a glance, before he throws it down on the table.

'Cheeseburger for me,' he says.

'You've got the specials, can you read them out?' says his mam, eyeing the piece of paper in front of him.

Tommy ignores the request but hands the paper to her. I watch Tommy out of the corner of me eye, fiddling with his cutlery. Probably the first time in months he's held metal knives and forks.

'So how are you feeling?' asks Dad, smiling at Tommy. Funny, but he seems nervous too, playing with the corner of his menu.

'Happy,' says Tommy.

'I bet,' says Dad, laughing, despite the lack of a joke.

'We're just so glad to have you home,' says his mam, looking teary-eyed, and grabbing Dad's fingers to stop them fiddling.

Everyone's looking awkward. Apart from me. Not sure why. Tommy gets to live with his mam again. Dad gets to live with his lass. I get to live with two people I hardly know, one of whom's been in prison. But I've moaned enough about it to Dad. The moaning got me nowhere. Just got to get on with it, he said.

So here am I, Ryan Dyer, having an odd lunch, getting on with it.

'What was the scran like… inside?' I ask, turning to Tommy.

'He means food,' says Dad.

'Crap. We mainly had takeaways.'

I blurt out a laugh.

Tommy recoils as his mam gives him a kick under the table.

'Was there much bullying among the young offenders?'

'I was classified as a juvenile offender,' corrects Tommy, 'as in juvenile delinquent. I was in Feltham A. It's like a creche for criminals.'

'Oh.'

'And yeah, there was bullying, and no, I wasn't bullied,' he says, emphatically, as if he's had enough of me questions. And probably me.

'Can we talk about something other than prison, please?' says his mam, shuffling in her seat.

It's the only thing I want to talk about. Need to find out what the real Tommy Cavendish is like. His mam says how great he is. If he's that belter how come he got banged up? Feel scared. And excited. The confusion isn't far behind.

'What's that on your front?' asks Tommy, squinting at me T-shirt.

I stretch the material so the letters don't get scrunched.

'*Skolstrejk För Klimatet.* It's Swedish for school strike for the climate.'

Want Tommy to think I can be a rebel too.

'Oh, yeah,' he says, 'saw that on TV. All those little kids moaning about the weather.'

Should have worn a plain T-shirt.

'Ryan's really into the environment,' says Tommy's mam, smiling at me, then him.

'Yeah, always checking to see things are in the right bins,' says Dad. 'And we don't eat too much meat.'

'And we don't leave many lights on.'

Please stop.

'Someone came to Feltham and gave a talk about sustainability.'

'That's nice,' she says.

'Not really. Some of the guys got bored out of their brains and a fight broke out.'

I laugh, although from Dad's expression should have kept it to meself.

The young waitress reappears, with an iPad.

'Would you like to order some drinks?'

'Orange juice for me, please,' says Tommy's mam.

'Tap water for me,' says Dad.

'And me,' I add.

'Pint of Becks, please.'

'Tommy.'

'What?'

'You're not eighteen yet.'

'Can't help that. Can't help feeling thirsty either.'

His mam looks exasperated. Feel sorry for her. She's had seventeen years of this to put up with.

Make that sixteen and a half.

'Okay, let's split the difference,' says Tommy. 'Bottle of Becks, thanks.'

'Can I have a Becks too?'

'No, Ryan, you cannot,' snaps Dad.

'Why not?'

'It's against the law.'

'Why is it against the law for me, and not for Tommy?'

'The answer is no.'

Dad can be annoying when he wants to be.

The waitress gets bored with the argument and lopes away to get three legal drinks, and one illegal. Tommy's mam looks down at the tablecloth and shakes her head. She was probably glad he was inside. Finally got some peace and quiet. Dad gives her a smile and places his hand back on hers.

Wonder what *my* mam's doing now. Could be in a restaurant somewhere with a new boyfriend, gazing into his eyes, holding hands, kissing, ordering champagne. But she's most likely sitting in front of the telly, plate of cheese and crackers on the armrest. Seething.

The waitress returns with the drinks and puts them on the table. Can't believe they let him have lager, while I'm stuck on tap water. Don't want to feel angry but can't stop meself. Things have got worse and worse since the divorce. Mightn't have been so bad if they'd stopped at that. But Dad went and got a job down in London. No one asked me what I wanted. I end up moving all the way down south, starting a new school where I don't know anyone, living with two strangers in a house I hate.

'Cheers,' says Tommy, raising his beer.

I clink his glass, but me cheer stays buried.

Arresdet

Never thought I'd miss this room.

But I did. Missed it every day. And every night. Especially the nights. Those long hours when you've got nothing to do but think about where you are, and who you are, and what you've done. Got too much for some of the guys. I'd hear them. Crying. Even hard lads, who'd stab their own granny for a fix. Now as soft as window putty. Not up for the role of hard man. Just kids. Wanting their mums.

It was the little things I missed most. Like going downstairs to get a Coke. Grabbing my skateboard. Playing my guitar. Or going down the hall to the toilet. Saying goodnight to Mum. The things I thought I'd miss, I didn't. Like my phone. And the mates who turned out to be anything but. Not that I was going to say no to my phone. Mum gave it to me when we got home.

'Please be careful, Tommy,' she said, with that look she's got.

'It's only a phone, Mum.'

'Not the phone I'm worried about. It's the people inside it.'

Knew what she meant. There were some in there who definitely need deleting. Not good for my soul. Not good for my health.

I'll do it. Some time.

Open it up.

Tons of messages. But none from the person I want.

Message her.

I'm out. U in? x

Press send and pray. Then pray a bit more.

Lie back on my bed. The mattress feels good, like a mattress should. Different from the pizza-thin one I've had beneath me all these months. Look around. The room is full, an Aladdin's cave. My clothes, posters, guitar, skateboard, games console, school stuff. It's also home to something else. A memory. The worst type. I don't want to dig it up, but it's still alive, like the monster that refuses to be killed. It's in this room where it all began.

It had been an average sort of day. Wouldn't end that way. Been skateboarding with a few of the guys. Hardflips, toeflips, railside, the works. Man, I was flying. Came home. Mum was in the back garden, planting in the flower bed. Had lunch. Toasted sandwich, I think. Though it could have been scrambled eggs. Went to my room and got horizontal. Headphones on. Chillin'.

Then it happened.

Crash. Crash. Crash.

Amazon deliveries never get that angry. Nor the postie. Whoever it was clearly didn't like our door knocker.

Crash. Crash. Crash.

Sat upright. Heart banging.

Loud voice through the letterbox.

'Open up. It's the police.'

WTF.

Should have rolled with it, strolled downstairs, opened the door and said, 'Okay, stay cool. I'm your guy.' But I'm not hard-wired that way. Didn't have my phone, or debit card, or jacket, or shoes. Things that matter mean jack at times like this. Had an escape route though. Chucked off my headphones, leaped off my bed, ran down the landing, through Mum's bedroom, out of the window, over the garage roof, grabbed the drainpipe, eased myself down, dropped to the ground.

Mum must have seen me land.

'Tommy,' she shouted.

No time to look. No time to explain. No time to breathe.

'Stop,' blared a copper, standing at the back fence.

The alleyway was no longer on my escape list. But Mrs Granger's garden was. Vaulted her fence and ran towards the next. Cleared that too. I was at the end of our street. All I had to do was... exactly what, Tommy? Run through the park? Steal a car? Rob a bank? Buy a jet? Fly to South America? Have plastic surgery? Steal an identity? Start a new life as Rafael Gomez? Hard to think straight when you've got a bunch of coppers chasing you.

Thought at least I'd make it to the park. Didn't make it to the nearest lamp-post. Taken no more than a couple of steps in my bare feet when someone who loved double cheeseburgers landed on top of me, sending me sprawling. What little air I had left inside was knocked out. My right arm went where it's not meant to go. Felt the bite of cold metal on my wrists.

'Tommy Cavendish, I'm arresting you on suspicion of...'

I lay there, gasping, as he went through his little speech.

Said nothing.

It was game over. The end. Curtains. Finito.

In another way, it was just the beginning.

Moved my head and saw a load of neighbours who'd come to watch. Some people don't get enough excitement in their lives. Didn't give a stuff about them. Only person I cared about was on her knees in the garden.

They dragged me to my feet. Some young lads started taking photos on their phones.

'Oy, paparazzi, back off will you,' boomed Officer Cheeseburger.

'Can you take me straight to the station?' I asked.

'We're taking you home first.'

'Don't wanna go home.'

'Not sure you're in any position to argue, young fella.'

The old Tommy, the pre-handcuffed one, might have persuaded them. But he's gone. This was the new Tommy Cavendish, accused of a crime he most certainly committed.

They took me down the alley, past the gawpers, the grinners, the gloaters. The closer we got to our house the louder it became. The sound of crying.

'Just put me in the car, will you?' I pleaded.

But they didn't care.

One of them pushed open our garden gate and led me in. There she was, sandwiched between two police constables. My mum. Never seen her with a face like that. Never want to see it again. Fear. Anger. Disgust. Sadness. Shame. The jackpot of bad emotions.

She rushed over and grabbed me, staring deep into my eyes, as if she was trying to see through me.

'What have you done, Tommy? What in God's name have you done?'

Teh crminial

'How's it gannin', pet?'

By 'it' she means them.

'Alreet, Mam.'

Her face beams at me from the screen. It looks like she's in a supermarket. Mam calls me about five times a week. I've never got much to tell her. Studying for me GCSEs. Seeing me mates. Watching Netflix.

But this week is different.

'Are you managing to keep away from him?'

'We live in the same house, Mam.'

'I'm not stupid, Ryan,' she sighs. 'I divvent want you getting dragged into anything untoward.'

Mam likes words like that.

'He's a different age, got different friends, goes to a different school. I don't think I'll be top of his list for new gang members.'

'I know. But I'm your mam, Ryan. I'm allowed to worry.'

Since she found out Dad's girlfriend's son was in prison, it's been her favourite topic of conversation. One I am already bored with.

'So what's he like?'

'Tall, slim, black hair.'

'No, as a person?'

'Mam, I've only known him twenty-four hours.'

'Cleaner to aisle five. Cleaner to aisle five.'

Definitely a supermarket.

Mam brings her face in close, as though she's letting me in on a big secret. 'Ryan, I want you to tell me if does anything, you know...'

'Untoward.'

'Aye, untoward.'

So bored with this conversation.

'Need to go, Mam.'

Even though I don't.

'Bet she's happy.'

'Who? Tommy's mam?'

'Aye.'

'Seems glad to have him back.'

'Oh, to have your son return home.'

Mam's never stopped being bitter about what Dad did.

'Well, mustn't keep you. Love you so much, Ry.'

'Yeah, love you too, Mam.'

She disappears to carry on shopping.

Feel sorry for Mam. Lost her husband. Her home. And now she's lost me. She argued like mad about me staying in Northumberland. But guess Dad was a better arguer. After the split, she went to live with her mam and dad in Coventry. Seems everyone is where they don't want to be. Apart from Dad.

Need to think about someone else.

Spot the perfect candidate.

I head into our small back garden. Tommy's lying on an air bed, earphones in, soaking up the sun. Prison is not the place to go if you're looking for a tan. Tommy's body is very long, very lean and very white.

Can feel me heart beating hard, as I stand over him.

Conversations are like plastic explosive. They need to be handled carefully.

'Hi, Tommy.'

'Hi,' he grunts.

'Did you take part in any riots?'

'What?' he says, taking out his earphones.

'Did you take part in any riots?'

'No.'

'But there's always riots in prison.'

He ignores me.

Maybe Tommy's not the rioting type.

'Did you attack anyone?'

'No, Ryan, if I did that I'd still be inside.'

'So what did you do?'

'Nothing.'

'But what was it like?'

Tommy sits up. He seems hacked off.

'Ryan, have you ever played cricket?'

Shake me head.

'Well, that's what prison's like. Long moments of boredom, until you face the fast bowler. Then it's total terror. That's prison – dull and dangerous.'

Note to self. Never play cricket.

'What's the worst thing you saw inside?'

'Ryan,' he says, getting up. 'When you've had a really crappy day at school do you want to talk about it?'

'Na.'

'Precisely. Prison was made up of one crappy day after another. Days I don't want to go over, least of all with you.'

With that he storms off into the house.

That did not go as planned.

Imagine when I get back to school, I'll be the centre of attention. For once. The guy who's living with a criminal. Everyone will want to know about it. But Tommy is batting all me questions away. On top of that he's not done anything remotely criminal. Apart from ordering a bottle of lager.

I've only made a couple of friends since I moved down south. Hoped Tommy might add himself to the list. But doesn't look like he wants anything to do with me.

Lie down on his airbed. Close me eyes and open me thoughts. I'd love to find a time machine and go back a year. Make it two. Me, me mam, me dad. Not this new line up. Don't do cooking but hear it's all about the blend of ingredients. Same with families. Ours is all wrong. Like ice-cream and cabbage.

Hear the kitchen door squeak. Open me eyes. It's her. Gotta stop calling her 'her'. Tommy's mam's got a name.

'Okay, Ryan?'

'Yeah... Gnome-y,' I say, trying it out for size.

'It's Nay-owe-me,' she says, 'three syllables.'

She sits on the grass next to me.

I get up and make a move towards the house.

'Can you stay a second?'

Sit back down on the airbed.

This is going to be a Tommy talk. I can tell.

'This must be difficult for you, Ryan. It's the same for Tommy. Having someone new in his home.' She looks over at the garage roof, a sad expression on her face. 'Believe me, he's not the guy you think he is.'

'You're saying he's innocent?'

She shakes her head and plucks a blade of grass from the soil. 'No, Tommy was guilty all right. But he's served his time. He deserves a second chance.'

'Sure.'

'He has his good points, and his not so good points, like all of us.'

'Sure.'

This is like one of those talks you get at school about relationships and stuff. So dull you learn to yawn with your mouth shut.

'I've had a very long chat with Tommy, and he promises me he's not going back to those old ways.'

'Sure.'

Must be a word other than 'sure', but not sure what it is.

'I understand this is strange for you, Ryan. Away from your old house, your friends, your mum. I can never replace her, but if there's anything you want to talk about, anything at all, I'm here for you.'

Don't want Three Syllable Naomi to be me replacement mam. Want the one who used to read to me every night when I was younger. The one who used to quiz me before exams. The one who used to buy me chocolates when I'd done well. And even when I hadn't. The one who was always there, even when I didn't need her to be.

She gets up and touches me shoulder.

'I know you're going to be a good influence on him, Ryan.'

Wouldn't be so sure of that.

Hedmastear

'What's he want to see us for?'

'Dunno, Tommy,' says Mum, as she drives carefully around a corner as though we're on black ice. 'Said he needs to talk, that's all.'

Feels weird going back to Hamilton. Not that I haven't seen any teachers. Men and women came into Feltham all the time. There was Mrs Roberts who taught me art. Loved those sessions. For a while I could forget I was locked up, and let my mind go places my body couldn't. She said my work was outstanding. Even if it wasn't, it made me feel I wasn't worthless. Then there was Mr Richards, our English teacher. Never been into books, but he introduced me to audio. For me, that's the perfect way to get through a story, get someone else to do all the reading for you.

Mum pulls into a space in the car park, right over a line. Not that it matters during the school holidays. We get out and walk towards the school.

'You must tell him about all the studying you've been doing,' she says, putting her keys in her bag.

'Yeah.'

'And the latest books you've been going through. What are you listening to at the moment?'

'*Life of Pi.*'

'Yeah, tell him that. And how you're going to stay away from the others.'

'I have to Mum, it's part of my licence.'

'Tell him anyway.'

'I know how to play the game.'

'Don't say that, Tommy. Whatever you do.'

Yes, Mum.

'I should have brought some of your art.'

'Mum, it's not parents' evening. He just wants a chat.'

Was glad it was still the holidays. Didn't fancy walking in with half the school staring, the other half taking photos. Some things you don't want to be famous for.

It's him, the one that got nicked.

If there's one thing worse than carrying out a crime, it's being caught for carrying out a crime. Feel like I've got a massive tattoo on my forehead – LOSER.

Spot a can on the ground. Take a big run-up and belt it as hard as I can. It goes clattering over a wall.

'Tommy, will you behave yourself!'

Only a can.

'Sorry.'

We walk into the main reception. There's a woman walking towards us. Mrs Jeffries, my old geography teacher.

'Hello, Tommy,' she says, surprise lighting up her face.

'Hello, Mrs Jeffries,' I mutter.

'Come to see Mr Watson?'

'Yes,' says Mum.

'Well, good luck with everything.'

And with that Mrs Jeffries goes scurrying off to her car.

We walk through the empty reception, up the stairs, through two sets of doors, and arrive at our destination: Mr Derek Watson, Headmaster.

Mum smiles at me and knocks.

'Come in.'

I open the door. Mr Watson is sitting behind his desk. He's on the phone.

'Won't be late. Chicken pie sounds lovely. See you soon, darling.'

He hangs up, gets to his feet and shakes Mum's hand, then mine.

'Thank you for coming in Mrs Cavendish, Tommy. Please take a seat.'

We sit in the chairs opposite him. Mum begins fiddling with the strap of her handbag. My right knee starts bouncing, no matter how much I tell it to stop. Look at Mr Watson's face. It goes from smiley to un-smiley in record time.

'I'm afraid there's no easy way to say this, but Tommy can't come back to Hamilton High.'

'What?' exclaims Mum.

'We had an emergency meeting with the school governors, and it was felt it's best if Tommy doesn't return.'

'Best for whom?'

Want to get up and leave.

But Mum's only just started.

'Why didn't you tell us earlier?'

'We've been reviewing the situation since Tommy was convicted.'

'Thought he should have got longer, did you?' she snaps.

'That's not what I said.'

Mum runs her hands over her face. 'I've been paying school fees, exorbitant fees for years, I've been a class rep, I've helped out on the Christmas Fair committee, stalls, fundraising...'

'This isn't about you, Mrs Cavendish. We're not denying you've helped our school considerably, but Tommy has been convicted of a crime, a serious crime.'

'For which he's served his time. Whatever happened to forgiveness?'

'It's not a question of forgiveness.'

'So what is it? You think Tommy's going to lead other boys astray? Going to rob the school tuck shop? You've got a duty to Tommy, to help him finish his education.'

'We also need to consider the good of the school.'

'What about the good of Tommy?'

You tell him, Mum.

'He's also got a Youth Offending Worker, Mrs Bridges...' she says.

'Mrs Brighton.'

'That's the one. She'll make sure Tommy stays on the right path.'

'Our decision is final, Mrs Cavendish.'

Mum might as well be talking to a chair.

'Turn around, Mr Watson, and read that sign,' says Mum.

Behind the Head's head is a large wooden plaque engraved with three words. The school motto. He doesn't bother to turn.

'It says, "Every child matters". Not just those who've never put a foot wrong. Every child.' Mum squeezes her bag even tighter. 'I know he's not perfect, but Tommy's tried hard here. He's not a bad kid. He needs another chance.'

The Head looks away, refusing to lock eyes with Mum.

'You're only bothered about the smart kids, aren't you? Those who get the top grades, make you look good in the school reports. Keep your fees high. You haven't got time for people like Tommy.'

'As you know only too well, Tommy has been a disruptive influence in class almost from the day he got here.'

Wondered how long he'd take to get around to this.

'But Tommy said he's going to knuckle down. Didn't you, Tommy?'

'Yeah.'

The Head drums his fingers on his table. He's heard enough.

'I'm sorry, Mrs Cavendish.'

She continues to glare at him for what seems like for ever.

'Come on, Tommy, let's go.'

I pick up a photo from his desk. It shows Mr Watson, a middle-aged woman, and three teenage kids. Looks like they're at a wedding. I imagine hurling it at his stupid motto, smashing that picture into a thousand pieces. But I promised Mum. I promised her. Take the deepest of deep breaths, put the photo back on his desk and get up slowly from the chair.

'Enjoy your chicken pie.'

Frist dya at scoohl

Can't believe what's happening.

I'm walking to school with Tommy Cavendish.

We haven't spent much time together over the summer holidays, but all that's about to change. We're not only in the same house, we're in the same school, the same class. He's been put back a year because of his gap half-year. In prison. Three Syllable Naomi said she'd decided to take him out of Hamilton. Said he needed a new start. His new start has started with me. Our lives are converging.

'You dead nervous, Tommy?' I ask.

'Spent six months with a load of nutters. Reckon I'll cope with this place.'

Tommy has the cool gene. Laid back, nonchalant, couldn't care less, like those gangsters you see on TV, who've got it all, and don't care what happens to them. Bullet-proof.

'Were you in a gang in prison?'

'For eff's sake, Ryan, can you shut it about that.'

Thought he might be prepared to talk more, now that

we have something in common. But Tommy does what Tommy wants.

We carry on walking, with only the sound of our shoes for company.

'How d'ya get that scar on your head?' he asks.

'Had a big fight with some guys in Year Nine.'

Actually got it falling off the stage in primary school during *The Lion King*.

If Tommy's impressed by how I got me scar he keeps it well hidden.

'You like school, don't you?' he says.

'What makes you think that?'

'Your polished shoes, bag full of books, tie done up, the fact we're early. That sort of stuff.'

Don't want him to think I'm a total nerd.

'I'm not always early.'

Tommy laughs.

He's right, though. Mam drilled these things into me from the first day I went to primary school. *Costs nowt to be turned out nice,* she used to say.

We're nearly at the school gates. I feel taller just being with him. I'd told me two mates Josh and Aiden that Tommy is coming. Explained where he'd been and what he'd done. Sent a screen grab of an article about the trial. Me phone was instantly filled with wide-eyed emojis. Reckon by the time Josh's spread the word, Tommy will be a mass murderer, who killed his victims with a flame-thrower, then ate them.

As we walk across the playground heads turn. Female heads. As if he's stepped straight out of a boy band. Tall, muscly, with hair too wild for any comb. He's the type I reckon girls throw themselves at. Never had that problem. If you can call it that. Although I am *with* Tommy. Which must count for something. I'm no longer a biological irrelevance.

Tommy spots someone at the gates and goes over.

'Hi, Tommy.'

'Hi, Mitch.'

They fist-bump.

Only Tommy could go to a school where he doesn't know anyone. And know someone.

'What you doin' here?' asks Mitch. Whoever he is.

'Climbed over the prison wall. Decided to hide in the first school I came to.'

Mitch laughs.

'This is Ryan, my new cellmate, sorry housemate.'

'Mitch,' says Mitch.

'Hi,' I say.

'When d'you get out?'

'Few weeks back,' says Tommy. 'They wanted me to stay longer, but I had a Get Out of Jail Free card from Monopoly.'

He laughs and slaps Tommy on the shoulder. 'Man, you crack me up. Which class you in?' asks Mitch, ignoring me, the way people do.

'What is it, Ryan?'

'Eleven C.'

'Eleven?' says Mitch, scrunching up his nose as though there's a bad smell. 'You got pushed back a year?'

'Yeah.'

'Bummer. Heard from Logan?'

For the first time Tommy doesn't seem quite so cool.

'No, he's still inside,' he mumbles.

'How come he didn't get out when you did?'

'Got a longer sentence.'

Mitch nods.

'Gonna catch up with him when he's out?' Tommy peers down at his shoes and shakes his head. 'Thought you two were mates.'

'Yeah, well, times change, don't they?'

Think Mitch realises he's stepping on dangerous ground.

'Well, see you round,' he says.

'Sure.'

They fist-bump again and Mitch strolls away, swallowed up by a group of lads by the bins.

'How do you know him?'

'Mitch is the cousin of a guy I knew.'

'Who?'

'Someone. No one.'

'I'll show you where the lockers are.'

We walk into school. Feel like Moses, with Tommy as the wave-parting machine. Seems everyone steps aside to let us through. Not used to that. I'm used to being invisible. I know it's not because of me, but for a moment I pretend that it is. I soak it all up.

Teh meteing

If you look like a victim, you become one.

One of the best bits of advice I heard in Feltham. Stand tall, be strong, even if your insides have turned to custard. This is how I act as I walk down our street. Not sure it goes down well with our neighbours. See a woman I recognise. She crosses the road when she sees me coming, like I'm infected. Spot Mr and Mrs Granger, in their front garden. They used to be quite friendly. They stare at me, then turn away quickly as if caught in a spotlight. I know they're talking about me, the guy who vaulted their fence and landed in juvenile offenders.

He's out already, you know. Thought he'd get longer.

Wonder if he'll bring his gang round here.

What am I meant to do? Stay home every day? I've as much right as them to live here. And I've been punished. Want to tell them a single bad decision doesn't make you bad. But what's the point? They've made their narrow minds up. Once a wrong 'un, always a wrong 'un.

Carry on walking, down streets where they don't know

me. Should feel more relaxed. I'm not. Still worried I might do something wrong. I know I've got a temper. Need to keep it buried deeper than radioactive waste. *Be of good behaviour.* That's what my licence condition says. All it takes is one slip. Every time the doorbell goes, reckon it's the police, come to take me back. Every time a police car goes past my heart skips a beat, thinking they're looking for me.

Not the only thing I'm worried about. Add my new school to the list. Thought I'd be anonymous. But seems everyone knows about me. Heard some crazy rumours about stuff that happened in Feltham. Who knows where they got that from? I confronted Ryan, but he denied it. He shows no sign of getting bored with me. Always by my side, like a shadow, even when it's not sunny. Guess he'll get fed up, and people will get bored of looking at me, as if I'm some sort of exhibit. But right now, I'm the top attraction.

Until then, I need to stay out of trouble. For me. For Mum. But easier said than done. When my fear and frustration get too much, disruptive Tommy comes out to play.

Make my way into the park.

I see her and wave. Doesn't wave back. Either hasn't seen me or doesn't want the world to know she's seen me. She's on a swing, long ginger hair draped over her shoulders, knees peeking out through holes in her jeans, slender hands gripping the chains. I walk up to her, smiling.

'Hi, Sprout.'

'Hi, Dish.'

Good to see at least our nicknames have survived.

Sit down on the swing next to her.

'When d'ya get your nose pierced?'

'Few months back.'

'Suits you.'

'Thanks,' she says, with that smile of hers, the smile I took with me into Feltham. I used to count down the days to when I would see it again, for real. And here it is.

I push off from the ground, which sets the swing moving. Alice pushes off too, matching the arc of my swing.

'I missed you,' I say.

If this were a movie she'd reply, 'I missed you too,' and we'd kiss and hug. But it isn't, so she doesn't. Instead she swings back and forward, staring into space.

'How was it?' she asks, softly.

'Not the best holiday I've been on. Jacuzzi got a bit crowded. And the discos were rubbish. Girl to boy ratio was terrible.'

From her expression today's not the day for jokes.

'You're an idiot, Dish.'

Can't argue with that.

'Hear you're at William Caxton.'

'Who told you that?'

'Not a lot happens around here. You're still news.'

Nice to know I'm good for something.

'You didn't reply to my calls.'

Only had two numbers cleared by the prison. People I was allowed to call. One of them was Alice. The calls all went to voicemail.

Hi, Sprout, it's Dish. I'm so sorry for what I did, and what I've done to you. Missing you so much. I'd love to talk to you some time. Really would. I'm so sorry. Miss you. Love you.

I left eighteen of those. Before I gave up.

She takes her time replying.

'I couldn't, Tommy.'

Pretty sure why. Her parents. They never put the welcome mat out for me. Too much of a loose cannon for their high-flying daughter. Prison was their perfect told-you-so moment.

'Do they know I'm out?' She shakes her head. 'Gonna tell them?'

Alice brings her swing to a halt with her trainers. 'No, Tommy, I'm not. As far as they're concerned it's over between us.'

'What about you?'

She runs her fingers through her hair. 'I've spent the last few months getting over you. I don't want to have to get over you again.'

I look across the park at a couple walking hand in hand. Glad when they finally disappear behind a café.

'Why didn't you tell me what you were up to?' she asks.

'You'd have been in trouble too if you'd known.'

'No, I wouldn't, because I'd have stopped you. I'd have made sure you didn't get involved. What on earth were you thinking?'

That's been my number-one exam question. *Tommy Cavendish, what on earth were you thinking?* Came up with a few suggestions. The buzz. The money. The friendship. The danger. Not sure any of them are right.

'I don't know, Alice.'

'Who's to say you won't do it again?'

'Me,' I say, loudly. 'I'm done with it. With them. I'm not going back inside.'

Alice looks far from convinced. Wish I could make her believe I've changed. But would I stand by me after what I'd done? Probably not. I'd shown I could go behind her back, and the backs of all the other people who trusted me and do something so stupid I was locked up. Leopards and spots. Leopards and spots.

'They won't even hear your name at home. Always had their doubts about you. Don't worry, I'd say, he's a great guy. And then you go and do that. How do you think it made me feel?'

'I'm sorry.'

She rocks gently on her swing.

'Me too.'

I reach for her hand.

She turns away.

'I'd like to try again,' I say.

'That's never gonna happen.'

'Why not?'

'Because I'm seeing someone else.'

Teh reqeust

'What's up, Tommy?'

The reply, if there is one, is too quiet to pick up.

'If there's anything you want to talk about, I'm here for you.'

'I've got my mum for that.'

'Of course. But if she wasn't around.'

'Why wouldn't she be around?'

'She might be out.'

'Then I'd wait for her to come back.'

Don't think Dad's little chat with Tommy is going as well as he'd hoped. Bit like me and Three Syllable Naomi.

'Want you to know me offer still stands. I'm here for you. Whenever.'

How come Dad never talks to me like that?

'Maybe we could go for a bike ride some time?'

'Maybe.'

Sense their conversation, if you can call it that, is coming to an end. Sneak back down the corridor to me bedroom and quietly close the door. Sit at me desk and spread books around as though I've been busy.

A knock.

'Come in.'

The door opens.

'Remember you've got your piano lesson at 7.30,' says Dad.

'Not gannin',' I reply, in A flat.

'What do you mean?'

'Too much homework.'

Hear me bed squeak as Dad sits on it.

'Ryan, you always have piano on a Tuesday.'

'Not anymore.'

A puff of air escapes his lips.

'You're going to give up your lessons, after all these years, just like that?'

'Yep.'

'Why?'

'Said. Too much work.'

Another large exhale.

'Does your mam know about this?'

'Nope.'

'Well, I'll let you break that one to her.'

Dad's disappointment fills the room like gas. The bed squeaks again as he lifts himself off it.

'If you've got any other big decisions, any chance you might tell me first?'

Maybe.

'Look, I'm sorry the way things turned out. For you. But they are what they are. And there's no going back.'

Wish he hadn't said that.

'I'm giving up piano.'

The bedroom door opens and closes. I stretch my arms and grin. Not the most rebellious thing ever, but it's a start. Been fed up with me lessons for ages, but never found the courage to stop them. Until now. With Mam away at Gran's, and Dad wrapped up with his girlfriend, it's the perfect opportunity.

Close the books I wasn't reading and make me way to Tommy's room.

He's lying on his bed, headphones in, staring at a cobweb.

'What's this, visitor time at Cavendish Prison?'

Ignore him and drop onto a bean bag.

'What you listening to?'

'I *was* listening to *Noughts and Crosses*,' he says, switching off his tablet.

'Cool.'

'I've given up piano.'

'Fascinating. You can go now.'

Not until I've said what's been nudging me brain for days.

'Do you know how to drive?'

'Yeah,' he mumbles.

'Will you teach me?'

Tommy props himself up on his elbows, and stares at me.

'You're kidding me, right?'

'No. I've driven once. But I want to get better. I want to pass first time when I'm seventeen.'

'Get your dad to teach you.'

'Said I'm too young.'

'He's right. Driving a car isn't the same as a computer game. It's serious. And anyway, I haven't got a car.'

'You could steal one.'

'Are you completely effing mad? I've been released from prison on licence. If I do anything wrong, and that means anything, I'll be returned quicker than you can say boomerang.'

'Okay, can you borrow one?'

'No, I can't.'

I spot another form of transport.

'Can you teach me skateboard tricks, then?'

Tommy seems lost for words. Reckon I'd make a good interrogator. Me questions have finally worn him down.

'Have you tried it before?'

'Aye, couple of times,' I lie.

'Okay,' he says, 'but ask your dad first. Not taking responsibility for anything going wrong.'

Cretaive wrtiing

I tie Ryan's shoelaces. Think he's enjoying his little power trip.

'Sure you two don't want a lift to school?' says Mum.

'No, we're canny,' says Ryan, not giving me the chance to speak. Would've loved a lift.

I grab his bag, slinging it over my shoulder.

'You can be the first to sign my cast,' says Ryan, smiling, as if he's proud of it.

Grab a pen from my backpack and write *Tommy*.

'Can you add Cavendish. There's a few Tommys in school.'

This kid gets weirder by the day.

Add my surname, and we walk out of the front door.

Ryan broke his left arm trying a jump at the skatepark. Told him not to do it. Problem is, he'd been watching me do tricks. But I've been skateboarding for years. Don't reckon he's ever been near one. Mum and Mark went crazy with me when we got home. Found out he'd never asked his dad if he could go.

We spent three and a half hours in A&E.

'What on earth did you take him skateboarding for?' groaned Mark.

''Cos he wanted to.'

'So, if Ryan asked to base jump from a tower block you'd let him?'

'He's sixteen years old.'

'And you're seventeen. Expect a bit more responsibility from you, Tommy Cavendish.'

'Don't take orders from you. You're not my dad.'

That shut him up.

Could have dropped Ryan in it. From a great height. Could have said how he wouldn't listen to my instructions. Was trying things way beyond him. Refused to wear a helmet. But kept my mouth shut. Like all good criminals.

At least I'm slowly getting used to the new school. The first week lasted a month, but as each day passes, can sense the interest in me waning.

'What delights has WC got for us today?' I ask, as we head towards the bus stop.

'Biology. Maths. Geography. Double history,' says Ryan, rattling off the day's timetable. 'First up is double English.'

Could do without that. Even an eighth of English would be too much.

We carry on towards the bus stop.

'What happened to your dad?' asks Ryan.

Since he'd run out of questions about prison, suppose it was only a matter of time before that one came up.

'He's not here.'

'So where is he?'

'Dunno.'

'Have you not tried to find him?'

Ryan's questions are starting to bug me. Decide to tell the whole story, what little there is of it, to save him asking any more. 'Mum had a one-night stand with a guy she met in a bar in London. Mum finds she's pregnant. The result is me. The end.'

'Didn't she try and track him down?'

'No, she didn't. She'd had a bit to drink. In the morning he'd gone. Had no contact details.'

'Would you like to find him?'

'And how do you suggest I do that, by wandering all the bars in London with an old photo of my mum, asking middle-aged guys if they remember her so I can tell them I'm their son? No, Ryan, think I'll give that one a miss.'

Right now, Mum's all I need.

To put a stop to Ryan's endless questions, I put my headphones in. We finally join the hordes shuffling into William Caxton. Follow Ryan to our class. All the guys are drawn to his broken arm, wanting to know what happened. Sure he'll fill them in with some ridiculous story that's about ten miles from the truth. I find a place at the back, tucked behind a heavily built Asian lad. Take a deep breath. Feel more scared about the next two hours than I did trying a railslide at the skatepark.

The teacher, Mrs Phelps, comes in. She's a woman with a voice that seems as if it belongs to a much bigger body.

'Morning Eleven C,' she hollers.

'Morning,' comes the high-pitched reply. Mostly from the girls. The boys haven't even noticed she's arrived.

She unpacks her briefcase and begins patrolling the room. 'Okay, can I have a bit of hush, please. I set you a creative-writing assignment, "Desert Discovery". Hopefully you all had fun tackling that.'

The faces around me say otherwise.

'The task gave you lots of opportunity to show your creative flair. You had the desert to play with and all the descriptive possibilities that offers, the searing heat, the scorched earth, the barren terrain, the cold nights. Then you had the element of surprise. A discovery. What was it in the desert that you or your protagonist had come across? A hidden mine? A remote property? A body, perhaps?'

'A KFC.'

Sniggers.

'Thank you, Thompson. Try to steer your mind away from chicken just this once.'

Mrs Phelps continues her patrol. 'I'd like to hear some of your responses.'

Stay away from me. Please, stay away from me.

I try to become invisible. But it's not easy when you're six two.

And new.

'What's your name again?'

She's standing next to me.

'Tommy. Tommy Cavendish.'

'Great. Could we hear your creative piece, Tommy?'

'Ur, left my laptop at home, Mrs Phelps.'

'Steal another one,' comes a voice.

Sniggers.

'Please,' barks Mrs Phelps. 'Okay, maybe we'll get to hear it next time.'

Mrs Phelps carries on cruising in search of desert tales. Grip the edge of my desk, my knuckles turn white.

The two hours drag. As only English can.

Finally, it's over.

'Well, thank you, everyone,' says Mrs Phelps. 'I have an assignment for next week. I'm aware how easy it is to get stuck in one genre, so I'd like you to pick a title from the library. The sort of thing you wouldn't normally read. And choose a section from this book. We'll look at some of these and see how different writers approach the art of storytelling.'

Class ends. Ryan comes over to me.

'What's up, Tommy?'

'Nothing. Why?'

'Your laptop's in your bag. I saw it.'

Brkeon

'Hello, Mam.'

'Hi, Ry,' she says, with a grin almost too big for me phone.

Can tell from the paintings on the wall Mam's in Gran and Grandad's dining room. They moved down to Coventry from Tyneside to be nearer Mam's sister, Alison. She has four kids. Mam only has me. Alison wins. Mam's other sister, Clara, lives in America. Not sure Gran would ever move there.

The Midlands is probably the perfect distance for Dad, and the worst distance for Mam. They rented out our old house in Northumberland, but don't think they make much from it. Mam didn't have any money to fall back on, so Gran and Grandad said she could stay with them till she got herself sorted. Seems the sorting is still going on.

'What's me baby been up to?'

'Usual. School. Homework. Stuff.'

'You're looking pale, Ry. Are you getting outside enough?'

'Aye.'

'Has she got plenty vitamins in?'

'Aye.'

Mam has that worried expression on her face.

'Show me that room of yours again,' she gans.

I give her a high-speed tour with me phone.

'Slower, Ryan, slower.'

What's this? Cell inspection?

'It's so titchy.'

The same size as when I showed you last week. And the week before that.

'And so messy.'

That's because it's hard to put stuff away with one arm.

'Does she not clean your room?'

'Naomi,' I say, stressing all of her syllables, 'expects me to do it.'

'Does she not know you've got GCSEs coming up?'

Doubt I'm going to fail me exams because I have to tidy away a few socks. But can't be bothered arguing.

I was going to tell her about putting a stop to me piano lessons, but I'll save that for another day. Got a bigger hurdle to jump over.

'Mam, got something to show you.'

I raise me plaster cast into shot. Mam slaps a hand to her mouth.

'Oh, my God. What on earth happened?'

'Skateboarding.'

'That is such a dangerous sport. Almost as bad as trampolining. Did your dad buy you one?'

'No, I used Tommy's.'

'But you've never tried it before. You need lessons.'

'Tommy was teaching me.'

Mam looks horror-struck. 'Well, he made a pig's ear of that, didn't he? Should have known that boy would get you into trouble sooner or later.'

'It wasn't his fault.'

'Course it wasn't. That boy is always innocent.'

Two large blue earrings sway as she continues to shake her head.

'How are Gran and Grandad?' I ask, trying to steer her down a different path.

'This is terrible, Ry,' she says, ignoring me question. 'What with your mocks and the effort we've put in.'

We?

'How are you going to study with a broken arm?'

'Me arm's in plaster, Mam, not me brain. And it's me left, so I can still write.'

'But you can't type.'

I learned to touch type years ago. I'll have to make do with one hand.

'I'll be fine, Mam.'

Her face is far from satisfied with me response.

'I should never have let your father take you down there. Knew no good would come of it. I should have stopped him.'

Can see Mam's upset.

'It's okay, Mam. Me arm'll mend.'

'It's not your arm, Ry. It's everything. Your father tells me this lad now attends the same school as you. In the same class. The cheek of it. Dropped it into conversation like it was no big deal. *Be good for Ryan to have some company*, he said. Company like that we can do without. A miscreant. If I had the money I'd find you another school tomorrow. And now this.'

'Mam, I asked Tommy to take me skateboarding.'

Seems to deflate her sails. Slightly.

'He's toxic. I want you to stay away from him. Do you hear me?'

'Aye.'

But just because I hear you, doesn't mean I have to obey you.

In teh sptloight

Some days you wish never got started. Grey skies to go with the grey streets and the grey faces. Thoughts of Alice and her new guy, on repeat. Images of Logan battering down my door. Carrying Ryan's bag. A day of lessons I'd love to swerve. At times, I'm tempted to return to my old ways. Never tried free-climbing, but imagine the buzz is insane. Ten cracked fingertips between you and oblivion. Until you make a mistake.

But I made a promise to myself in Feltham.

This is the one and only time you are coming here.

People say I'll be back. As if it's inevitable. Like gravity.

Need to prove them wrong. But it's hard. Wish I was more like Piano Man, with his predicted grade nines, his highly polished shoes and his glowing reports. Always been allergic to school, but I'd like to change. I should ask him for help. He's always around. Know I won't. Help is something I've never asked of anyone. It's a sign of weakness. Maybe that's what's happening to me. I'm becoming weak.

'When my plaster's off, will you take me skateboarding again?'

'No. Your dad will kill me, and if he doesn't, my mum will, and if she doesn't, your mum will.'

Ryan shrugs, as if me being killed is no big deal.

We walk past The Magpies.

'Can we gan for a drink ?' asks Ryan, looking at the pub.

'Three problems. It's 8.20 in the morning. We're in school uniform. And you look about thirteen.'

'I meant later. I could wait in the beer garden.'

'No.'

'Can you help me get fake ID?'

Maybe that fall off the skateboard broke his brain too.

'Yes, I can get a fake ID. No, I'm not going to get you one. Do you want to get us both into trouble?'

He shrugs again.

'Go back to your piano. It's safer.'

Ryan thinks life is a game. Where no one gets hurt.

He doesn't ask me any more stupid questions.

The day I wish had never started gets a little bit worse. First subject. English.

For Mrs Phelps's assignment I went to the school library and took out *Paddy Clarke Ha Ha Ha*. No idea what the book's about, but it sounded funny. Could do with a laugh right now.

I look for a desk near the back, somewhere safe to hide. But all the best spots have been taken. End up sitting behind a girl who's small in all departments. Hasn't even got big hair.

The door opens and Mrs Phelps appears.

'Morning, Eleven C,' she bellows, dropping her briefcase heavily onto the table.

'Morning, Mrs Phelps,' comes the high-pitched reply.

The guys are busy talking football.

'Okay, can we have some quiet, please?' The muttering becomes a murmur. 'Last week I asked you to choose a book from the library that was different to the sort of thing you normally read. What did you choose, Liam?'

'The Bible.'

'Well, that's certainly different. Wasn't quite the sort of story I had in mind. What about you, Cassie?'

'*Lord of the Flies*.'

'Excellent choice. A book that was originally turned down by every publisher William Golding sent it to. The author went on to win the Nobel Prize for Literature. It just goes to show, writing isn't simply about talent, it's about perseverance.'

So want this lesson to end.

'Today I thought we'd get you to read extracts from the books you've chosen and explore the approaches the authors have taken.'

Some of my old teachers used to ask if we were okay reading out loud. Not Mrs. Phelps.

'Now, who shall we start with?'

Wish the girl in front would have a growth spurt. But she remains as small as ever. Feel like a soldier in a trench that's nowhere near deep enough, about to be shot in the head by a sniper. Sweat begins to break free. My hands feel clammy. My mouth is as dry as a litter tray. Please ask someone else.

Seems my luck's in. Mrs Phelps goes to the far end of the classroom, looking at the books on display.

'Tommy didn't get to read last week,' comes a voice from the front of the class.

Ryan.

Why the hell would he turn the spotlight on me?

'Yes, be good to hear from our new arrival,' she says, smiling.

Need to think of an excuse. *Forgot my book, Mrs Phelps*. But the book is there on my desk, looking up, laughing at me. *Tommy Cavendish Ha Ha Ha*. Want to get up and run away. But look what happened last time. I used to get out of stuff like this at Hamilton by messing around. Got me into trouble. But got me out of having to read. Promised Mum I'd behave myself at my new school. That I was never going to get thrown out again.

I'm trapped.

Mrs Phelps walks over. From the corner of my eye I see her standing next to me. Thought this morning's porridge had long gone. Clearly not. Swallow it down.

'*Paddy Clarke Ha Ha Ha*. Very good, Tommy,' she says. 'Booker Prize-winning novel.'

Should have read it. That would have been the smart thing to do. It's not so bad when I've been through things a few times. But hadn't even opened it.

'Do you want to read the opening to the story, Tommy?'

No, Mrs Phelps, I'd rather cut my own throat with a blunt axe. Can feel everyone in the room staring at me, wondering why I'm waiting. Wouldn't be so bad if Ryan wasn't there. Whatever I say will go straight back home. To his dad. To my mum.

'Come on Tommy, we haven't got all day.'

Open the book with fumbling fingers. When I read in my head, any problems I come across stay in my head. They belong to me. But when I read out loud my problems become public, on show for the whole world to hear.

I'm scared, because some words are like landmines. Buried in the text. You think they're harmless. But they're not. They get you.

Bang.

'Come on Tommy, school finishes at four.'

But it's hard to speak when your heart's in your mouth. Gripping the book as tight as I can, I begin.

'We were coming down our road. Kevin stopped at a gate and bashed it with his stick.'

Feel the words coming out slowly, too slowly.

'It was Missis Quickly's gate...'

'It's not Quickly, it's Quigley,' says Mrs Phelps, looking down at the page.

Sniggers.

Reading and speaking is way too much for my brain. Wish she'd go back to the front of the class. She knows I can't do this. That's why she's here. Checking on me. Making it worse.

'Carry on, Tommy.'

My eyes return to the page.

'She was always looking out the window but she never did anything.'

'Sounds like some of you lot,' says Mrs Phelps.

'Quigley, Quigley, Quigley, Quigley, Quigley!' I say, finally getting into the rhythm of it.

Can see more names coming up. Want to ignore them. But can't. Not with her there, checking.

'Lana and Adrian turned down their coal-de-sac...'

'It's Liam and Aidan,' she says. Not in my head it isn't. 'And it's cul-de-sac. No such place as a coal-de-sac.'

Laughter pinballs off the walls. Other classes will be wondering what's so funny. Wishing they were in Mrs Phelps's lesson.

Can feel my leg begin to bounce, uncontrollably, as I try to read more lines.

'We said nothing; they said nothing. It'd be brilliant, wouldn't it? I said.'

Mrs Phelps sighs all over my hair. 'You've missed a line, Tommy. Liam and Aidan had a dead mother. Missis O'Connell was her name.'

'Think I might need glasses,' I say, floundering for an excuse, any excuse.

'Think you might be right. Well, seeing as Tommy's struggling a bit here, I suggest we move on. How about you, Fran?'

Mrs Phelps moves away. I release the book from my grasp, keeping my head lowered. My face is glowing from the blood that's rushed there. A tiny drop of sweat dive-bombs off my brow onto the page. Know they're all looking at me, wondering why a seventeen-year-old guy can't read *Paddy Clarke Ha Ha Ha*.

As Fran races through the first chapter of her book, my heart gradually slows, the heat from my face recedes, my right knee stops vibrating. But one thing doesn't diminish. My anger. Why did Ryan drop me in it?

Cnfrntatioon

What's up with Tommy?

He sounded so nervous. Never seen him like this before. Thought he was the type who nothing would ever phase. All Mrs Phelps asked was for him to read a few pages of a book.

At the end of the lesson, I go up to him, but he glares at me, and tells me to go away.

I can't go away. I live with him.

At lunchtime, he sits brooding over a plate of beans. I decide not to join him. He looks furious. Manage to avoid him for the rest of the day, but the last lesson is history with Mr Pike. Tommy's in the same class, at the back as always. Make sure I grab a desk near the front for a fast getaway. Sneak the odd peek at him. Still looks like he wants to kill someone. Don't want to walk home from school with him. Not today. I'll carry me own rucksack. Hope by tomorrow he'll have calmed down.

After an hour of hearing how Hitler murdered his way to the top, the school bell goes. Me stuff's ready in me bag. Grab it with me good hand and race for the door, as fast as I can. Dash doon the corridors, swerving around bodies, through reception and into the playground. Glance behind me. No sign of Tommy. Need to keep moving.

Leave the school gates and hurry up the street at a pace Dad would be proud of. Must be safe now. About to check when a hand grabs me blazer, spins me and pushes me into a tree. A knob of wood digs into me back. Tommy glares down.

'What were you doing back there?'

'W-what do you mean?' I stammer.

'Don't play the innocent with me, Ryan Dyer. You know exactly what I'm talking about. *Tommy didn't get to read last week,*' he says, in a high-pitched voice I'm sure I haven't got. 'Why the hell did you do that?'

'I didn't do anything wrong.'

'If you thought that why you been avoiding me all day, eh? Why did you shoot out of school like a rocket?'

''Cos you looked so angry. I only mentioned it because you missed out last week. I thought you'd like to'.

Tommy's so cool and confident, I assumed he'd be amazing at reading. Assumed wrong.

He lets go of me blazer and smooths out the creases he's created.

'Thought you were trying to stitch me up.'

'Why would I do that?'

Tommy shakes his head. 'I don't know. My head's just messed up right now, okay. I'm sorry.'

He looks up the street at some kids having a pushing match.

'Was it the fact the book was written in Irish?'

'No, it wasn't the fact it was written in Irish. It was the fact it was written with words.'

'Everything's written with words.'

'I don't want to talk about it, okay?'

What's up with him? He's clearly got an issue with reading. Why won't he admit it?

'You can get help.'

'I don't want help. Least of all from you.'

'But...'

'Shut the eff up,' he shouts.

Tommy clenches his fists, breathing hard.

Wait for the storm to pass.

'Was trying to do you a favour.'

'Favours like that I can do without.' He brings his face close to mine. His features blur. 'Don't ever try something like that again.'

'Of course.'

Tommy walks away.

A different Tommy from the one I knew yesterday.

Xplusioen

Drop my head onto the pillow.

Used to spend hours in Feltham, lying on my bunk, staring at the ceiling. I'm on a different bed, staring at a different ceiling, but the bad stuff is still there, like a permanent headache. Close my eyes and this morning's English lesson returns with all its sweat-inducing, leg-bouncing, hand-shaking horror. It's so raw I can feel it, like an open wound. I'm not like the others. I don't race through pages, I stumble, I trip, I fall. Humiliating.

Wonder whether to tell Mum what happened. The wondering doesn't last long. I've shovelled enough problems her way. And why tell her now, after all these years. This is for me to sort out. Although I haven't the faintest idea where to start.

I feel stupid for blaming Ryan. Not his fault I'm rubbish at reading. But I suppose the only good thing is I didn't lose my rag in school. Can forget about it and move on.

'Tommy,' shouts Mum, in a voice that chills me.

Something's up. That something is almost certainly me.

'Coming.'

Climb off my bed and trudge downstairs. If it is bad news, no point in rushing towards it. Open the sitting-room door. They're all there, with the sort of faces you see in hospital waiting rooms.

'Sit doon, Tommy,' orders Mark.

Find a stool and lower myself on to it.

'I had a call from one of the teachers at school,' says Mum.

My heart begins to pound. Mrs Phelps has been in touch. She's told Mum about my reading.

'Mrs Laytham said she saw something. Looked like you were threatening Ryan.'

Try to stop a laugh, but it finds a way out. 'Threaten him? Why would I do that?'

'Thought you might tell us,' says Mark.

'Why don't you ask Ryan?'

'He's not saying anything.'

Sure enough Ryan has his mouth closed, his eyes firmly fixed on his plaster cast, reading the names on it. It's both good and bad that Ryan hasn't spoken. Good that he hasn't said why I grabbed him. Bad that they'll want to know what on earth is going on.

'I didn't threaten him, Mum. I swear.'

'So, what did you do? Mrs Laytham said you grabbed his blazer and pinned him up against a tree.'

Know whatever I say will come out badly. But have to say something.

'We were just play fighting.'

'Six-foot-two Tommy, play fighting a boy with a broken arm?' says Mark, angrily.

'Aye,' goes Ryan, 'it was nowt.'

Their faces say otherwise. They think Ryan said nothing happened, not because he isn't being bullied, but because he is.

'Whatever is going on between you two, I want it to stop,' says Mark, in as high a volume as I've ever heard from him.

'Yeah, we can't have you thrown out of another school.'

See Mark's face darken. 'How many has he been thrown out of?'

Mum's eyes move to the street. Trying to avoid the question. But I know there's no ignoring it.

'How many?'

If she won't answer, I will.

'Four.'

'Four,' exclaims Mark.

'Yeah, two primary, two secondary.'

'How come no one ever told me this?'

Because it's got nothing to do with you.

'Let's talk about this in private, shall we?' says Mum, trying to calm things.

Mark looks at Mum with an expression that's hard to read. Anger. Sadness. Disappointment. Maybe all three.

Now would be the perfect opportunity to explain everything. That the reason I got thrown out of all those schools, apart from Hamilton, was because of the pain, the shame, the bullying. Being made to feel small because I struggled with things others found easy. But once again I roll a boulder in front of my mouth and keep quiet.

Mum and Mark leave the room.

'Thanks,' I mutter.

'What for?'

'For not dropping me in it.'

Ryan grins at me. There's something brewing in that super-sized brain of his. Something I'm not going to like.

Hlpeing hnad

Things have taken an interesting turn in the Cavendish-Dyer household.

Tommy thinks I deliberately dropped him in it with Mrs Phelps. Mrs Laytham, Three Syllable Naomi and Dad think he might be bullying me. And to top it all, I learn Tommy is running out of schools to be thrown out of. The last one came as a big shock. His mam told me he needed a new start. Never mentioned this was the school's idea, not hers.

Felt a bit scared at first. Tommy's clearly capable of causing trouble wherever he goes. But, apart from the tree incident, I've not seen much sign of this. Just stays in his room most of the time listening to audio books.

None of this would have happened if Tommy had owned up to his reading problem and got it fixed. But, for whatever reason, he won't. Or can't.

A few days after the family board meeting I decide to pay him another visit. He's adopted his usual position, headphones in, staring upwards, like a stargazer with a ceiling in the way.

'Y'areet?' I ask.

'Never better,' he lies, taking off his headphones.

I flop into his beanbag.

'You should have told your mam what happened during English.'

'I do what I like.'

Bet it was talk like that that got him locked up.

'Does she know about your reading?'

'Stop banging on about it, will you?'

Tommy's in one of those moods.

Tread carefully, Ryan.

'I can help you.'

'Don't want your help,' he says, scratching his curly hair. 'Though I wouldn't mind a bit with my maths homework.'

Knew he'd crack eventually.

'Sure,' I say, as confidently as I can.

Tommy tilts on to his side and looks at me, my body half-swallowed by beanbag. 'Thanks again for not saying what happened in class the other day.'

'Omerta,' I say, closing an imaginary zip across me lips.

'What's that mean?'

'It's a code of silence in the Mafia. Italian for close your gob.'

He nods.

Now's me chance.

'In the Mafia there's normally some sort of reward for your silence.'

'We're not in the Mafia,' he says.

'No, but you've been in prison.'

'Where are you going with this, Ryan?' says Tommy, the angry look back on his face.

'There are a few guys in our class who've driven a car. I want to be like them.'

More importantly, I want to do something more exciting than look at books. I want people to think there's more to me than high marks.

'Oh, not that again,' he says, dropping on to his back. 'Ryan, you've got a broken arm, and you're still only sixteen.'

'Time will deal with both of those.'

'I'm not gonna grab a car just so you can do some three-point turns.'

Guess that's that then.

Like a ninety-year-old boy, I extricate meself from the beanbag. Tempted to go back to me room. But I made him a promise.

'Shall we take a look at this maths, then?' I say, moving across to his desk.

'Yeah,' says Tommy, sitting up.

'And me offer still stands with helping you to read.'

'What makes you such an expert?'

'Because I'm dyslexic too.'

Dxlsyesia

'Are you saying I'm thick?'

'Said nothing of the sort.'

'Thought dyslexics were the dumbos in class.'

'I've got dyslexia and I'm doing okay.'

'So how come I'm not?' I say, kicking a trainer across the floor.

'Cos you haven't had it checked out, man. I mean, look at you, you're brilliant at art, sport.'

Sounds like my mum talking.

'You went to private school. How come they didn't spot it?'

'Maybe I'm also brilliant at hiding things.'

Didn't do a very good job of hiding it the other day.

'So what's your dyslexia do?' I ask.

'It affects me reading cos the right hand side of me brain is dominant.'

'So half your brain can read, and the other half can't.'

'Aye, Tommy, something like that.'

'So what happened to you?'

'I struggled. Slow reader. Rubbish speller.'

Been there. Done that. Got the T-shirt.

'So how come you got to be uber smart?'

'Dyslexia doesn't stop you being smart.'

'How did you get it fixed, then?'

'There was a teacher at our primary school, a dyslexia specialist. She put a learning programme together for me.'

'Like what?'

'It was a long time ago, but involved loads of stuff to do with breaking up words, matching letters with sounds, and recognising letter sounds in words.'

'And that cured it?'

Ryan laughs.

'No. When I got to secondary school they taught me organisational skills, how to revise, essay writing, stuff like that. Me dyslexia's still there. But it doesn't get in the way.'

Ryan's right about loads of things, but he's wrong about this. How can words that don't make sense one day, suddenly make sense the next?

But, then again, what if he's right? What if I could use one of those learning programmes and read and write like him? Stupid idea, Tommy. You're seventeen. Only got a couple more years at school. Not enough time to get yourself fixed.

Not surprised Mum never picked up on it. At every school I went to my reading and writing were the least of their problems. Remember parents' evening. Top marks for art and PE. The rest of the time was taken up by my behaviour. Think Mum spent all her energy just trying to keep me from being thrown out.

'Talk to your mam about it.'

'No,' I snap. Fed up of talking about reading. 'You gonna help me with my maths or not?'

Over the following days Ryan helps me out. The numbers, equations and graphs slowly start to make sense. I keep reminding him not to tell Mum or Mark I've got extra tuition. He does as he's told. I'm grateful. But should know there'll be a price to pay. No such thing as free study.

On the day his plaster cast came off, he walks into my room.

'Look, two arms,' he says, waving them in my face.

'Great. You can take up boxing again.' He laughs and sits down on my bed. 'Ryan, wanna say thanks for the help you've given me.'

'No probs.'

'I owe you.'

As soon as the words are out I realise they should have stayed in. Can almost hear the cogs in Ryan's brain whirring.

'There is something.'

'Oh, please not that.'

'Yeah, that,' he says, grinning. 'I've driven a car before.'

'You've got two arms again, would you like a guitar lesson? I can teach you the main chords?'

'No.'

I'm worried about Ryan's request. I've got my provisional licence, but he hasn't. What if we get caught?

Not exactly what you'd call good behaviour. But then driving up and down a deserted road is hardly criminal. Not like I'm robbing an armoured car or anything. And it only has to be one lesson.

But it still makes me nervous.

Ryan can be so stubborn. I know he's gonna bang on about it every single day.

'Okay, I'll give you a bloody lesson.'

Teh drviign lsseon

'Two teenagers up early on a Sunday morning, what's the world coming to?' says Three Syllable Naomi, munching a slice of toast.

'Off to watch a football match at the rec,' says Tommy.

'Didn't think you were a football fan, Ryan?' she says, looking over the top of her reading glasses, the Sunday papers spread out on the table in front of her.

Before I have time to manufacture a lie, Tommy beats me to it.

'A top local team, Blue Star Rangers, are playing this morning. Thought I'd show Ryan what he's missing.'

Not even sure there is a team called Blue Star Rangers.

'Think I'll come too,' says Dad, detonating our plans.

'The boys don't need you cramping their style,' she says. 'Any road, you always go for a bike ride on Sunday morning.'

Dad leans against the fridge, slugging an energy gel. 'Yeah, watching twenty guys chase a leather ball versus forty miles' worth of fresh air? Bike wins.'

That was close.

We grab our coats and walk to the train station car park. Tommy looks twitchy, walking around in little circles, blowing out clouds of air.

'Whose car you borrowing?'

'An old mate from Hamilton,' he says, clapping some warmth into his hands. 'Belongs to his elder brother, Sam.'

'He's just gonna let you borrow it?'

'Know Sam well. He trusts me.'

'What about me?'

'We do not breathe a word that you're going to drive, okay?'

'He'll be in the car, won't he? He can't fail to spot I'm driving.'

'Don't panic. Told him I need to practise my reversing. He said he'll go for a run and see us later.'

Feel me stomach begin to scrunch. Perhaps I shoulda asked Tommy to teach me something else. But I so need this. Got a text from Mam last night asking how me schoolwork was gannin'. As if that's all I am, a study machine. But Mam's not here. Nor is Dad. Need to take me chance.

Before me nerves get totally shredded a small blue car speeds into the car park and comes screeching to a halt next to us. A young guy in running gear jumps out, and fist bumps Tommy.

'Good to see you, bro,' says Sam.

'Yeah, been too long.'

'Who's this?' says Sam, eyeing me suspiciously.

'Oh, it's Ryan, my mum's boyfriend's son. He's come along for the ride.'

'He wants to watch you reverse?'

'Ryan loves cars.'

Sam stares at me as me heart goes up several gears. Think any second he's going to ask me the engine capacity of different four-by-fours.

Feel I'm about to be sick.

Sam throws Tommy the keys. 'Enjoy,' he says. 'Gonna do a few laps of the park. Back in about twenty.'

'Cool.'

Sam turns and runs off at a pace I couldn't keep up for ten seconds. We watch until he's disappeared from sight.

'Okay,' says Tommy, 'get in.'

Come on, Ryan, man, show Tommy what you can do. I've been watching driving videos on YouTube all week, and practising under me desk, with books for pedals and an umbrella for the gear stick. Hope it's as easy as it looks on screen.

I climb into the driver's seat.

'Cannit reach,' I say, stretching me legs as far as nature will allow.

'That's because you haven't adjusted it, you dingbat. There's a lever on your side.'

I find it and shuffle the seat closer to the pedals. There wasn't a YouTube video for seat adjustment.

I check the gear stick's in neutral. But can't see where to put the key.

'There's a slot at the side of the steering wheel,' says Tommy, sighing.

I find it. Turn it.

A throaty sound escapes from under the bonnet.

I've actually started a car.

After a bit of fiddling I manage to find what could possibly be first gear.

'Okay, now slowly ease your left foot off the clutch, and depress the accelerator gently with your right.'

'I know what I'm deein'.'

Feel the car inch forward.

'We're moving,' I shout, triumphantly.

'Yes, Ryan. That's what cars do.'

After a couple of failed attempts, and some strange grinding noises I find second gear. We are now moving at a speed not far off Sam's jogging pace.

'This is brilliant, Tommy.'

'Thought you'd done this before?'

'I have. But it's still brilliant.'

'Yeah,' he mutters, clearly not sharing my enthusiasm as we crawl along at thirteen miles an hour.

I drive to the end of the car park, find reverse, turn the car around, and head back again. Tommy yawns. This must be his most boring Sunday morning ever. Having gone up and down a few more times, Tommy checks his watch.

'Sam'll be back soon. Don't want him to catch you behind the wheel. Reckon we have one more run.'

I've used less than half the gears. Doesn't seem fair. Want to go faster.

'I'd like to get into third.'

'Okay,' mutters Tommy, 'take it slowly and steadily. No sudden movements.'

I press the clutch and find first. A bit of acceleration. Find second. A bit more acceleration, and after some fiddling with the gear stick, I'm there.

'We're in third.'

'Must let mission control know.'

'This is so much—'

Before I can form the word 'fun' another car enters the car park. We're in a section that narrows. There's barely room for two vehicles. I'm moving towards it quickly. Too quickly.

'Change down,' shouts Tommy.

Suddenly need all me concentration for steering. Can't do anything else.

The car gets closer.

'Stay to the right,' bellows Tommy.

I steer in that direction.

The car is almost upon us.

'I said right,' he screams.

But his instructions are all wrong.

We're so close I can see the terror in the eyes of the other driver.

It's too late.

I crash into the other car.

Teh accdeint

Bang.

The horrible sound of metal head-butting metal. I lurch forwards. Lurch backwards.

The other driver turned her wheel at the last moment, avoiding a head-on collision. But the damage is done. We've crashed Sam's car.

'Damn, damn, damn.'

Ryan is open-mouthed, eyes popping, arms dead straight, gripping the steering wheel, like some sort of teenage zombie.

'Run, Ryan, run.'

But he's been hypnotised by what's happened. I unclick his seatbelt and elbow him in the ribs as hard as I can. Ryan snaps out of his trance, and opens his door. I leap out, snatching a look at the middle-aged woman behind the wheel. She seems okay. Apart from the sobbing. And the mangled wreck of her car.

I race towards the woods. Glance back. Ryan is rooted to the spot, gawping at the crash, as if trying to make sense of what he's done.

'This way, Ryan,' I scream.

He begins to move, but years at the piano stool have done nothing for his fitness. I run back, grab him by the arm and drag him towards the trees.

'For crying out loud, move.'

He stumbles along beside me, panting heavily. We reach the woods, where we both come to a stop, hands on knees, sucking up whatever air we can find. My head is full to the brim with bad thoughts. I pluck one. Sam. What am I going to tell him? Pluck a second. What the hell is he going to do to me? Then another hits me.

'You've never driven a car before, have you?'

'I, ur...'

I grab Ryan by the scruff of his sweatshirt. 'Tell me the truth.'

'No.'

Let him go. He cowers from me.

'Why the hell did you lie?'

''Cos you'd never let me in the car.'

Can't believe he'd do that. Just to find third gear.

'You told me to turn right into the other car,' says Ryan.

I think of the two cars heading towards each other. Me shouting instructions. The wrong ones. A wave of embarrassment breaks over me. Feel like Mrs Phelps is standing next to me, not Ryan.

'Why did you say "right"?' pants Ryan.

I kick at a stick.

'Guess, because I'm dyslexic too.'

Ryan squints at me from behind his glasses. 'What's that got to do with anything?'

Big breath.

'I get my left and right confused.'

'Why didn't you say?'

'Because we're in an empty public car park at nine o'clock on a Sunday morning. I didn't think it would be an issue. And just because I said turn right, didn't mean you had to go and do it.'

'But this was a driving lesson. I thought you knew what you were doing.'

'And I thought you knew what *you* were doing. This is your fault, Ryan. You're the one who said you could drive. You're the one who insisted on driving.'

'You made me crash.'

Curl my fists.

Ryan cowers.

I'm an ace away from hitting him.

But an image of my old cell appears.

My fingers unfurl.

I look back in the direction of the car park. It's only a matter of time before Sam returns, finds his crumpled car, and comes looking for us. For me.

'What we gonna do?' asks Ryan, in a voice shaking with fear.

'Leave it with me. I'll think of something.'

Gltuiy

Tommy's thinking doesn't amount to much.

'Let's go home,' he says.

I could have thought of that.

We trudge back through quiet streets.

Words are a waste of time.

Tommy finally takes out his phone. Luckily the person he calls isn't answering.

'Sam, it's Tommy. Look, mate, sorry about what happened to your car. Wanted to stay and explain, but had to leg it, because... well, you know, I'm on licence. Not meant to get involved in anything. I'll make it up to you, I really will. Speak to you later.'

Wondered why Tommy had shot off like he was in the hundred metres final. Of course, he's meant to steer clear of trouble. And I'd just steered us both into a ton of it. But Sam isn't the only problem. There's Dad and his girlfriend. What if they find out? Correction. What happens *when* they find out? It's impossible to hide something as big as a car. Sam knows what we did. The woman driving the car will have a description of us. There's probably CCTV in the car park. No way we can slither out of this one.

We reach the house. Our only consolation is that Dad's out on his bike. But that still leaves Three Syllable Naomi. We stand on the doorstep, steeling ourselves for the storm that's about to hit.

'What we gonna say?'

'Leave it with me,' goes Tommy, face full of intent. More than happy to do that. He's had more experience with things like this.

He opens the front door and I follow him through to the kitchen where we find his mam at the table, still working her way through the Sunday papers.

'You're back early,' she says, looking up from a colour supplement. 'Was the game cancelled?'

'There was no game, Mum,' says Tommy. 'We need to talk.'

We both slump down into chairs. Three Syllable Naomi closes her magazine.

'What's happened?' she says, gripping the edge of the table.

Tommy's Adam's apple bobs as he swallows the horrible truth. 'There's been an accident.'

'What sort of accident?'

'I took Ryan for a driving lesson.'

'You *what*? You told me you were going to watch football.'

The guilt is too heavy for Tommy's head and it drops

forward. 'I know I did, Mum. I'm sorry, really super sorry. But I promised Ryan I'd give him a lesson.'

Three Syllable Naomi's eyes swivel from Tommy to me. 'Why didn't you ask your dad?'

'I did. He said no.'

Feel like I could cry. But don't want to. Not in front of the Cavendishes. I want to be hard. Like Tommy.

'Whose car did you use? Tell me it wasn't Mark's?' she says. 'Please tell me it wasn't his?'

Dad's crazy about vehicles. When he and Mam split up, he replaced his screensaver of her, with a picture of his Lexus.

'No, it was Sam Fieldings'. Brother of a mate from Hamilton.'

'And does this Sam know about the accident?'

'Yeah. I spoke to him.'

'And what did Sam say?'

'Don't know. I left a voicemail.'

'So you haven't spoken to him.'

Three Syllable Naomi has turned into his prosecutor, tearing Tommy's flimsy story to shreds.

'And what did you hit?' she says, turning to me.

'Another car.'

'Parked car?'

'No, moving,' I mumble.

Her hand flies to her mouth. 'Oh, my Lord, was anyone hurt?'

'No,' says Tommy.

'Did you speak to them afterwards?'

'No, we ran away,' I say.

Tommy kicks me leg under the table. Shouldn't have said that, but then never been in a situation like this before. Feel miles out of me depth.

'So, if you ran away, how did you know the other driver was okay?'

'She seemed okay,' said Tommy.

Apart from the sobbing.

'Seemed?' says Three Syllable Naomi, in a voice growing ever louder. She folds her arms over her chest. Can sense her anger rising. Never been afraid of her before. But I'm afraid now. Bit like Tommy, don't know what she's capable of. She's not the only mam I'm worried about. There's mine. Told her I was revising all weekend. What am I gonna tell her? What will she do to me?

'You absolute bloody idiots,' screams Three Syllable Naomi. 'What were you thinking? Or rather *not* thinking? First you lie to me and Mark. Then you drive a car while underage, without insurance. And then, worst of all, you run away from the scene of an accident.'

'The driver was okay, Mum.'

'You don't know that,' shouts his mam, glaring at Tommy. '"Seemed okay" were your precise words. Did you speak to her? Did you get her to walk around to check if she was all right? No, you ran away like a couple of cowards.'

And this is only half of it. Dad hasn't had his say yet.

Tears begin pooling in me eyes. I'd be useless in a gang.

'I thought better of both of you.'

We lower our heads, like criminals in the dock. Guilty on all counts.

'What we gonna do?' says Tommy, his knee bouncing faster than ever.

'Grab your coats. We're going to the police.'

Bhavieour

Be of good behaviour.

I'd arranged for a teenager to drive a car, knowing he didn't have a licence. I wasn't qualified to teach him. Neither of us was insured. I'd run away from an accident. Can behaviour get much worse?

I blame Ryan. Why did he lie and say he could drive? Why didn't he ask his dad? Why didn't he just wait until he was legal? Why didn't he steer left when I told him to steer right? He must have known we were going to crash. Have I got that much hold over him?

I blame myself. Should never have agreed to Ryan's request. No matter how much homework he helped me with. No matter how quiet he kept about what he'd heard at school. No matter how much he banged on about it. I'm older. I'm meant to be more mature.

The person I feel most sorry for is Mum. I swore I wouldn't get into any more trouble. And here I am, in it right up to my neck. Will she ever trust me again?

Mark will be mad too. But don't really care. He's only her boyfriend.

Mum messages him. Another one straight to voicemail.

'Mark, it's Naomi. Some bad news. The boys have been involved in an accident. Don't worry, no one was hurt. At least I don't think so. Now brace yourself. Ryan was driving, with Tommy in the passenger seat. They ran away from the scene. I'm taking them to the police station. Call me when you get this.'

If Mark isn't red-faced after his bike ride, he will be when he hears this.

Mum drives us to the police station. I've never seen anyone stick so rigidly to the Highway Code, as if she's trying to make a point. Mirror, signal, manoeuvre. Indicating every turn, leaving loads of space between the car in front, at least five miles an hour below the speed limit.

I look across at her. Mum is as pale and old as I've ever seen her. The worry lines are lines I've drawn. The grey hairs have been put there by me. I've done this to her.

Check my phone. Three missed calls from Sam. Not sure I can handle him right now. Power my phone off.

'What do you want us to say?' says Ryan, in that little boy voice he saves for moments like this.

'The truth, Ryan. I want you to tell the truth.'

The one thing we've kept from Mum is how it actually happened. I'm glad Ryan has kept this to himself. Whichever way you look at it, neither of us comes out of it well. I asked Ryan to turn right when I meant left. And Ryan stupidly went right when common sense should have said go left. By obeying my instructions we ended up with the worst possible result.

Mum parks the car, ensuring she is perfectly between

the lines, and we walk in silence to the station. Behind the desk sits a menacing-looking police sergeant. Mum takes a deep breath and goes up to him.

'I'd like to report an accident.'

Mum tells the guy what's happened. Ryan, Mum and I are then shown to an interview room, where a young policewoman takes our statements. Ryan and I go through the whole story again. Ninety-five per cent of the story. The only bit that's edited is the crash itself.

'I just panicked when I saw the other car,' says Ryan.

The police officer seems happy enough with his explanation. Sixteen-year-old boy, first time behind the wheel, makes a wrong turn. Imagine they've got bigger fish to fry than the two sprats sitting in front of them. A young guy got stabbed outside a kebab shop two nights ago. Our little crash hardly registers.

Except in regard to me.

'What's going to happen to Tommy?' asks Mum, leaning forward across the desk.

'What do you mean?' replies the officer.

The shame and guilt from all those months ago bubble up to the surface.

'Tommy was released on licence from Feltham last July.'

The expression on the officer's face takes a turn for the worse. One of the young men in front of her isn't as innocent as he appears.

'I see,' she says sternly. 'That's for the Young Offenders team.'

Mum leaves our details and we go outside. She's okay. Until she gets into the car. It's too much for her. Having got me back, I'm on the verge of being taken away again. Tears begin their escape. I reach over and hold her hand.

'It's gonna be okay, Mum,' I say, without a sliver of evidence to back this up.

She says nothing,

I look at Ryan in the rear seat.

He mouths one word.

Sorry.

Lfet. Rghit.

Why didn't I ask for guitar lessons?

The police said they'll take a statement from the driver of the other vehicle and consider what further action is necessary. What does that mean? If they're okay we'll walk free and if they're hacked off we go to prison?

When we get back from the police station Dad's waiting for us, still in his cycling gear.

'Get in here, you two,' he says angrily, pointing to the sitting room.

Tommy and I troop inside. As if the crash wasn't bad enough, there's having to explain it over and over. Maybe Tommy's good at this sort of stuff. But not me. I'd normally be studying this time on a Sunday, not standing in our sitting room, feeling sick to the depths of me stomach.

'Mark, I've already given them both barrels.'

'Don't I get to have my say?' he shouts.

'Course you do. But there's no point in going over old ground.'

Not sure Dad cares how old the ground is. Seems only too happy to go over it again.

'Tell me what happened,' he booms.

Tommy tells him.

Minus the bit about left and right.

Dad walks around the room in his little black padded shorts, his cycling shoes clumping on the wooden floor.

'Can't believe this,' he says, unzipping his jersey to reveal a brown V shape, like a slice of pizza, on his otherwise white torso. 'Don't know what's worse. The lying, the driving, the crash, or the running away.'

'Sorry,' I mumble. But not sure he hears.

'And then there's the cost. How much damage was done? It could cost a small fortune.'

'Mark, it's only money,' she says. 'Tommy might get sent back to prison.'

From the look of horror on his face, don't think this had occurred to Dad yet.

'Oh, my God. What did the police say?'

She runs her fingers through her hair as she dredges for the information.

'If Tommy's deemed to have broken the terms of his licence, his manager makes a request to the Public Protection casework section. They'll decide if Tommy needs to be recalled, and for how long. If that's what they agree on, Tommy will be arrested and returned to prison.'

Dad doubles over as if he's been punched.

'All this over a stupid driving lesson.'

Dad flops onto a chair, breathing heavily, as if he's cycled up a hill in the wrong gear.

'So disappointed in both of you.'

Silence. Apart from the sound of cars in our street.

'Can I chat with these two?' says Dad.

Three Syllable Naomi nods, and leaves the room.

Dad sits for some time, gathering the thoughts he needs. He finally speaks, dividing his eye-contact equally between me and Tommy.

'You guys have both been absolute bloody idiots. You, Tommy, should know better. And you, Ryan, need to know that actions come with consequences.'

So want this day to end.

'What's important isn't so much the crash, but how you two respond to it. We all do things we wish we hadn't. But you've got to learn from it, and make sure you don't do anything like it again. Whatever happens after today, you both need to come back stronger, better. Do I make meself clear?'

Tommy and I nod.

And with that Dad gets up and leaves.

Tommy and I sit there, thinking about what's been said. And what's still unsaid.

Left. Right.

Tommy is never gonna forgive me for this.

'All I wanted was a bit of excitement.'

'Well, your wish came true, Ryan.'

Tommy gets to his feet, and walks across, towering over me. Can't bring meself to look at him. 'Because of what you did, I might be going to prison. So while you're sitting here at home, having pizza, drinking Coke, watching TV, I'll be banged up. Think about that for a moment.'

Reckon any second the blow is going to land.
But he just stands there.
'I wish I'd never set eyes on you.'

Msr Brghtoin

'Hello, Tommy.'

'Hello, Mrs Brighton,' I say, sitting down opposite her. I've worn my best suit. My only suit.

'What happened to your face?'

'Got a boot to the head, playing football.'

Got punched in the head by Sam Fielding.

He came to our house the day of the crash. Tried to talk my way out of it, but my talking let me down. Said I did most of the driving, and let Ryan have a go at the end. Said I tried to steer Ryan away from the other car. Said it was a total accident. Don't think he cared. I'd lied to him and let a virgin driver behind the wheel of his car. After being hit by a barrage of swear words I got hit by his fist.

Didn't retaliate.

Deserved everything I got.

Sam said I'd pay him whatever it cost to get his car back the way it was. Then after a load more expressions ending in 'off', he left.

'How have you been?' asks Mrs Brighton, as if we've just bumped into each other in the street.

'Been better.'

If possible feel worse than I did that day in court awaiting my verdict, because then I knew what the outcome was going to be. But now I'm balanced on a tightrope. On one side life, hope, choices. On the other side, prison. And Mrs Brighton has the power to push me whichever way she wishes.

'Not a great state of affairs, Tommy,' she says, knitting her fingers and staring at me. 'What made you do it?'

Been asking myself the same question, over and over. I need to give her a better answer than the one I've been giving myself.

'As you know, I share my home with a young guy, Ryan Dyer.'

Mrs Brighton nods.

'He'd been helping me a lot with my homework. Told him I was grateful, really grateful. He asked for something in return. Thought it might be a Nando's. Never thought he'd ask if I'd teach him to drive. Course I said no. I'm not old enough to teach. He's not old enough to drive.'

'You have a provisional licence, Tommy?'

'Yeah.'

'But you've never taken your test?'

'No.'

Mrs Brighton makes more notes.

'So Ryan was insistent about having a driving lesson?'

'Yeah. Going on and on about it. I thought why not give him one lesson. To shut him up. You know what I mean?'

From her expression, not sure she does.

'I knew a guy who'd lend me a car.'

'Did this guy know Ryan would be driving?'

My eyes take a left turn away from Mrs Brighton's.

'No, he didn't.'

'You lied to him?'

Big breath.

'Yeah.'

Bang goes another nail into my coffin.

'And where was this driving lesson?'

'The station car park. It was Sunday morning. Knew it would be quiet.'

'But not quiet enough.' She looks down at my report. 'And you, sorry, Ryan collided with another car. How did that happen?'

'Ryan was getting better. More confident. Thought we'd try getting into third gear. Then this other car appeared, at a part where the car park narrowed. Ryan panicked, and that was that.'

Mrs Brighton stares at me. 'Ryan turned into the path of the other vehicle?'

'Yeah. Not sure he knew what to do when he saw the car.'

'Wasn't it fairly obvious?'

'Not to him.'

'But you were the more experienced driver. Didn't you tell him what to do?'

Turn right, Ryan.

'It all happened so fast.'

Though not as fast as my heart now.

'And what about the occupant of the other car, a... Mrs Stocksfield. How was she?'

She knows the answer to this. She's testing me.

'I don't know for sure. Ryan and I ran away.'

'You ran away?'

'Yeah, know we shouldn't, but we panicked.'

Mrs Brighton continues with her nodding as she weighs up my answers. 'Tommy, your licence conditions require you to be of good behaviour, to not commit any offence. Do you feel you've met those requirements?'

This feels like the hangman giving you the rope.

'No.'

'No, neither do I. What you did was incredibly stupid and irresponsible.'

Which way is she going to push me?

'It's against the law to drive under the age of seventeen. It's against the law to teach someone if you're under the age of twenty-one. It's an offence to leave the scene of an accident.'

I feel myself slipping from the rope.

'Fortunately, you chose a quiet car park. The car wasn't stolen. Your intentions were not malicious. You weren't driving. And last, but not least, Mrs Stocksfield wasn't injured. Thankfully, your mother reported the incident to the police within twenty-four hours.'

I'm expecting a 'but' to arrive any moment. But the but is nowhere to be seen.

'It's for that reason that I won't be recommending we revoke your licence.'

She's pushed me the right way.

'Thank you, Mrs Brighton. Thank you, so much.'

She leans across her desk, eyeballing me. 'Don't get complacent, Tommy. If I see any repeat of behaviour like this, and I mean anything, I won't hesitate to put your licence under review. Do I make myself abundantly clear?'

'Yes, Mrs Brighton.'

She stands up and offers her hand, which I shake vigorously.

'Stay out of trouble, Tommy. Please.'

Mma vrseus Dda

'How are things, Ry?'

Feel like I did in primary school, when I struggled with me words, the way Tommy struggles now. Can't find a single one that works.

Shrug.

'There's something you need to tell me, isn't there?'

Her eyes squeeze tight. They look like two scars.

Dad's told her.

She knows.

'I'm sorry, Mam.'

'There's nothing to feel sorry for, pet. It's that stupid Cavendish kid's fault.'

Not what I was expecting. Thought Mam would be like Three Syllable Naomi and go crazy with me. But she's tipped all the blame on to Tommy.

'We were both responsible.'

'Divvent be daft. Who's the older of you two? He is. Who agreed to teach you? He did. Who got the car? He did. Who failed to grab the steering wheel at the critical moment? He did. I told you he'd be a bad influence and I've been proven right.'

I want to put her straight. Say I was the one who pressurised Tommy. That he didn't want to do it. That I was the one who crashed. But what's the point? She's made our minds up.

'I need to pay towards the repairs.'

'You'll do nothing of the sort.'

'And that's where you're wrong, Katie.'

Mam's eyes widen to their full circumference, as Dad turns the laptop in his direction, the camera now facing him.

'Tommy and Ryan were equally to blame. Ryan can pay his fair share.'

'Well, look who it isn't,' says Mam, sneering. 'Come to eavesdrop?'

'No, come to tell the truth.'

'That'll make a change.'

'Ryan needs to pay for what he's done.'

'What you've done, more like it. All of this happened on your watch, Mark. Where were you when this crash happened?'

'Cycling.'

'Exactly. None of this would have occurred if I'd been there.'

'Oh, you'd follow two young guys around day and night, would you?'

'No, but I'd set boundaries, house rules. And I'd make sure our son stayed as far as possible from that criminal.'

'Ex-criminal.'

'Don't give me that. Seventy-five per cent of juvenile offenders re-offend.'

Mam's been Googling again.

'He's a decent young man.'

Mum leans in so close to the screen I'm surprised she's not misting up the camera. 'If he's that decent how come you failed to tell me you were moving in with a woman whose son was in prison?'

Dad slumps back in his chair. 'Not that old chestnut again.'

'You kept it hidden because you knew it was wrong.'

'I didn't tell you because I knew you'd blow it out of all proportion, like you do with everything.'

'Mark, in case you hadn't noticed, that's our son sitting there, a son in his GCSE year. A son with very high predicted grades. We didn't agree on much except Ryan's education. That's why we helped with his dyslexia. Why we got him extra tutoring. I would never have let you take him to London if I thought he was about to share a home with a delinquent.'

Dad kicks the corner of my desk, making Mum wobble. First time in ages I've had a ring-side seat to one of Mam and Dad's fights. Wish I was further away. Another room. Preferably another house.

'I thought I could trust you to take care of our son. I was clearly wrong.'

'I am taking care of him.'

'Really? First you let this Tommy break our son's arm. Then, when Ryan crashes a car that Tommy probably stole, somehow our son is to blame.'

Dad reaches forward and presses the volume button, reducing Mum to three bars.

'The person to blame for all this is you,' she shouts. 'If he doesn't get the grades we talked about, I'll hold you personally responsible.'

Mum's face headbutts the keyboard as Dad slams down the lid on me laptop. He sits there, lips clamped, as he composes himself.

He puts a hand on me shoulder. 'Thought it might help me being here. You live and learn.' And with that Dad walks out of the room and closes the door.

The chat was meant to turn into a family discussion about the accident, and what to do next. It turned into another car crash. Mam and Dad arguing like crazy, not caring if I heard. Not bothering to ask what I thought. As if I'm invisible.

Thought there was always a wafer-thin chance they could get back together but seems that chance has finally gone. And I've played me part. I've done something I never thought possible, made Mam and Dad hate each other even more than they did before.

Maybe Mam's right. Should have stayed a million miles away from Tommy Cavendish.

Teh srpruise

Lyin' Ryan.

That's what I'll call him from now on. He told me he could drive. Yeah, maybe a CGI car on screen, or a dodgem at the fair. But as for an actual two-ton piece of metal, he's never come close.

He might be smart at history or physics, but he doesn't get real life, like what happens when you do something bad. He's got zero idea, as if prison is some sort of game, where no one loses. But it's been one big defeat; confidence, friends, relationships, they've taken an almighty battering. And just when I'm getting back on track, he nearly gets my licence revoked.

Decide to avoid him. Course, might bump into him on the way to the toilet, or down a corridor, but I won't speak to him. And that's how it goes. Day after day after day.

A few kids at school ask what's up between us two.

'Why don't you ask him?' I reply.

Mum and Mark notice. You'd have to be a lump of concrete to miss it. But neither of them says anything.

They know how much trouble he caused. And there's nothing they can do to fix it.

The bill for the two cars came in. Just over two grand. Sam's insurance didn't cover it as he'd let me use his car. Mark said he'd pay half, and the rest would come from Ryan and me. Got nowhere near enough to pay that. He said we could get jobs next summer, after our GCSEs, and pay him back. The thought of working all summer to earn nothing makes me hate Lyin' even more.

Money's not my only problem. Still have words to worry about. Mrs Phelps came up and asked if I needed help. Told her I was okay, that I got nervous reading out loud. Which is borderline true. Said I was getting through lots of audio books. Since then she's stopped asking me. But word clearly hasn't got around the staffroom, because sometimes other teachers ask me to read. If it's not too long or too tricky I manage to fluff my way through it or make a joke and worm my way out. I've also got other tricks. Developed a sudden sore throat, discovered an urge to go to the loo, forgotten the glasses I don't wear. But there are times when I can't escape. And humiliation sits waiting patiently for me.

One bright spot in this black week. Bump into Alice. I'd gone to a café to do some work.

'Flat white for Mr Cavendish,' she says, placing my drink on the table.

'Hi, Sprout, I mean Alice. Didn't know you worked here.'

'Didn't know you came here.'

'Don't normally. Fancied getting away from home.'

The café is quiet. Alice sits opposite me. She looks annoyingly good in her black shirt and trousers. But then Alice would look good in a bin bag.

'What's happening in Tommy-world?'

Decide not to tell her about the accident. It'll only make her think less of me than she does already.

'Not much. Eat. Sleep. School. Work. Football. Repeat. What about you?'

'Same. Minus the football.'

We both smile.

'You seeing anyone?'

Best joke I've heard in a long time. While there are plenty of girls at school who seem keen on me, can't be bothered being keen back. Too much going on. And none of them come close to the girl opposite me.

'No, I'm not. How are things with you and…' whoever he is.

'Fine.'

At least she didn't say amazing. That would kill me.

'How's your mum?' she asks.

Alice and Mum got on well. Think Mum was almost as disappointed as me when I told her it was all over.

'She's fine too.'

That's what happens when you split up. Small talk breaks out.

'Alice, can you clear the tables at the front, please,' shouts a guy I guess is her boss.

'Sure.'

Alice stands up. 'Maybe see you in here again some time.'

'Yeah.'

She leans over. I think she's going to kiss me. But instead she wipes some crumbs from the table and walks away.

I decide never to work in this café again.

I go home, thoughts of Alice trespassing. Need to move on, no matter how hard it is. Go through the front door and hear a woman's voice in the sitting room.

'Take a deep breath through your nose and go into downward dog.'

'Tommy?'

Open the sitting-room door. Mum's on a yoga mat in her workout gear, making an upside down V with her body, bum stuck high in the air. A woman on the telly is in the same pose, but better.

'Where've you been?'

'For a coffee.'

'Thought we might go out later.'

'Let's go into Warrior One,' says the woman on the TV.

Mum lets go of the floor and reaches for the ceiling, as if she's surrendered.

'Who's we?'

'You and me.'

'Where we going?'

'It's a surprise. A nice surprise. Reckon you could do with cheering up.'

'Now into Warrior Three,' goes the woman.

Mum balances on her leg, pointing her arms.

'I've got a match at one o'clock.'

'We'll go after that.'

Mum pauses the video.

'Ryan tells me you're in the school first eleven.'

For once Ryan isn't lying.

'Yeah.'

'I'm proud of you, Tommy.'

Although doesn't seem a big deal to me.

She walks over. Stops short of touching me.

'I know what happened that Sunday morning isn't you, the real you. It's difficult, but you have to try and let the past go.'

It's not the past that worries me. Lyin' Ryan is right here in the present.

Hoem swete hoem

Dad takes me to a Saturday afternoon screening at the cinema.

Think he's trying to build bridges. But he's made a strange choice for a peace offering. A war movie. As we sit in our seats, it dredges up a memory, Mam and Dad either side, me in the middle. Now it's Dad, me, stranger. Divorce does things like that.

The film takes me mind off things for a couple of hours. And while no one splits up, breaks their arm, or falls out over a car crash, lots of people get killed.

When the war is over, we walk back towards his car.

'How's it going between you and Tommy?'

You know exactly how it's going.

'The same.'

'Was a big shock for him, Ryan. He could have gone back inside.'

'Yeah, but he didn't, so there's nowt to worry about,' I say, a bit louder than I intended.

A tense silence as we head down the High Street.

'I need you two to get on.'

Need?

Had enough talking about Tommy.

'Can't we find our own place nearby? You can still see Naomi.'

Dad sighs so heavily, if it was his hundredth birthday every candle would have been blown out.

'No, Ryan, we are not doing that,' he says, disgruntled.

Only just changed school. Unless I want to move school again in me GCSE year and move up to Gran's, I'm well and truly stuck.

'I know it's not what you want, Ryan, but you've got to accept it.'

It is what I wanted. A friend. Someone to look up to. But not sure I can bear the next three years living with me own personal hater.

We get into the car.

'Got a surprise for you,' he says.

'What?'

'All will be revealed.'

We drive off. Count the turns. Five left. Three right. Dad finds third gear four times. Like doing that. Keeps me brain from thinking of other things.

'Here we are,' he says.

We've come to a halt outside a modern semi.

'Who lives here?' I ask, confused.

'With any luck, we will,' says Dad, grinning. 'Our offer's been accepted.'

There's a For Sale sign in the garden, a SOLD sticker slapped across the front.

No wonder Dad got so grumpy about me wanting to move out. He's gone and bought a place for all four of us.

'Why didn't you tell me?'

'Naomi and I wanted to keep it a surprise. Also, didn't want to build our hopes up. Sales can fall through.'

So can marriages.

'That means you've sold our old house.'

Dad nods.

Feel empty. Our old house in Northumberland was me final link to the past. And now it's gone. I used to love that place, with its thick stone walls, huge garden, and fields that went on for ever. Dad puts his hand on me shoulder. Maybe he knows what I'm thinking.

'It's gonna be a new start. For all of us.'

'Does Mam know you've bought it?'

'It's nothing to do with her.'

'Who's paying for it?'

'Naomi and I.'

'What if things don't work out?'

'They will.'

Bet he said that to Mam once.

'There are no solar panels.'

'We can get some.'

And then I spot something else. A few spaces further up the road, a car I know only too well.

'The Cavendishes are here.'

'I'm not asking you and Tommy to talk. Just look,' says Dad, elbowing me, 'you'll love it.'

Hate it when people make me decisons for me. But can tell how excited Dad is, the way he's jiggling his keys.

Want to stay in the car. But I've done enough recently to annoy Dad.

We get out and walk up the path.

Dad rings the doorbell. It's opened by a smartly dressed middle-aged woman wearing a ton of make-up and a banana-shaped smile. She's carrying a clipboard, like those charity people you get in the street wondering if you can spare a minute.

'Mr Dyer,' she says, offering her hand. 'And you must be...'

'Ryan.'

'Lovely to meet you. Come on in.'

We go inside. The house is totally empty. Like it's been burgled. By very keen burglars.

'I'll let you two have a look around,' says the woman.

Follow Dad into the sitting room, a dull space that me head has to work extra hard to fill with furniture.

Hear the sound of heels on wood.

Three Syllable Naomi.

Need to stop calling her that.

'Hi, Ryan.'

'Hi, Naomi.'

'What do you think?' she says, gesturing excitedly, as though there was something there.

'Good.'

'Fantastic, isn't it?'

'Fabulous.'

Battle of the adjectives.

We walk into the hallway. Tommy's there, wearing his football kit, minus the boots.

'How did you get on?' I ask.

'Lost.'

Can tell from his face the defeat is the disastrous variety. Before I can ask by how much Tommy hurries away into the kitchen, as if he's forgotten to turn the gas off.

I follow Naomi upstairs. She clearly knows where she's going as she walks down the landing and opens a door.

'This is going to be your room.'

I obviously don't have any say in this. I gaze around, even though there's nothing much to gaze at. Emptiness. But at least there's lots of it. I imagine me bed, table, chair, wardrobe, chest of drawers. Reckon there's still room for loads of other stuff I don't yet own.

'You're allowed to say wow,' says Naomi, grinning again.

'Wow,' I say, in me least wow voice.

'So much bigger than our place, isn't it, Ryan? There's even room downstairs for a piano, if you decide to take it up again.'

Which I won't.

Feel her hand on me shoulder. 'This can be the start of a whole new chapter.'

One Tommy probably won't even be able to read.

'Why don't you go explore?'

Don't want to. But not a whole lot else to do. I know sooner or later I'll come across Tommy. Sure enough, I find him in a study, or dining room, or TV room. Hard to tell what rooms are meant to be when there's nowt in them.

'What do you want?' he snaps, arms folded across his mud-spattered jersey.

Even though me tongue is sick of the sound of it, I say it again.

'Wanted to say sorry.'

'Apology rejected.'

And with that he disappears to look at more empty rooms.

The prposoal

Happy for Mum.

She's never had a proper boyfriend before. Certainly not a serious one. Most of them didn't last longer than a snowman.

Gonna see him again, Mum?

Not sure.

Meaning 100 per cent sure.

She'd put her perfume away for a few months, until the next one. A conveyor belt of possibilities. But it changed when Mark appeared. When I first saw them together on visitor day it would be little touches, like you see with kids at school, wanting to give affection, but not wanting to be seen showing it. When I got home from Feltham it would be kisses. Now they've moved to the clinging phase. All that's missing is a neon sign above their heads saying – *We're in luuurve*.

I'm at my desk doing some work. Trying to do some work. Wish I was more like Lyin' Ryan. He rattles through every assignment in the blink of an eye. I sometimes wonder if we've been given the same homework. Even though I did study in Feltham, it's nothing like being in school in GCSE year. There is *so* much to do. But I need to try and get decent grades. Show Mum I can do more than draw and kick a football.

Decide to open a book. But they're waiting for me. The words that are the wrong shape to fit into my head. I stare at them, but staring doesn't make it easier. They're not friends of mine. Never have been. Trying to trip me up. Slow me down. Make fun of me. I start reading, but it's like eating soup with a fork. Only a bit goes in.

There's a tap at the door.

'Come in.'

Mum.

There's a question been eating at me.

'You're moving 'cos of me, aren't you?'

'What you talking about?'

'The neighbours.'

'We are *not* leaving because of them, Tommy,' she says, putting every kilo of her weight behind the word 'not'. 'Their reaction may not have been what I'd hoped for. But the truth is, we need more space. As for the people out there, I couldn't care less about them.'

'What about our new neighbours?'

'I'm not going to lie to them. People will find out. But they'll see you for who you are, a decent, hard-working, talented young man.'

Who can't read properly.

'Anyway, I didn't come up here to talk about them. I'd like you to come downstairs.'

'Why?'

'Come and find out.'

Happy for the interruption, I close my book and follow Mum to the sitting room. Mark and Lyin' Ryan are already there. Mum takes a place on the sofa next to Mark. I grab a stool and sit as far from Lyin' as possible. Press my hands on both knees to stop them coming to life.

'Suppose you're wondering why we've called you here,' says Mark.

From his expression he's feeling pleased with himself. He clasps Mum's hand, and they look at each other lovingly.

'We're going to get married,' they say, in unison.

Shocked. Like when you're watching a game and a goal comes out of nowhere.

Pleased for Mum and Mark. Not so pleased for me. Unless they get divorced, I'm going to be wedded to Lyin' for ever. But can't let this tip iced water on Mum's big moment. I jump to my feet and hold her tight.

'That's great news, Mum.'

'Thanks, Tommy.'

Go to shake Mark's hand. He ignores it and goes for the full-on bear hug.

'Well done, Mark.'

'Cheers. I'm a lucky man,' he says, patting my back, as if I had something to do with it.

Lyin's a little slower on the uptake. He wanders across, as though he's handing in homework that's half-finished.

'Well done,' he says.

Mum hugs him, and he hugs her back. He breaks free and hugs his dad.

One big happy family. Mum and Mark stare at each other as if they can't believe what they've done.

'When's the big day?' I ask.

'We're getting married at the end of January,' says Mum, squeezing Mark's hand. 'When your mocks are over.'

'How come you've not gone for the summer?'

'We want to get on with it,' says Mark, beaming. 'And venues are a lot cheaper in the winter.'

'Hope you two are as excited as we are,' says Mum. 'Or just half as excited.'

'Yeah,' I say.

'Aye,' goes Lyin', without much enthusiasm.

'Think this calls for a little something,' says Mark, who leaves the room and reappears with a champagne bottle in one hand and four thin glasses in the other.

He puts the glasses on the coffee table and starts fiddling with the foil.

'Couldn't believe it,' says Mum.' We were in Sergio's, when Mark, in front of all those people, gets down on one knee, a rose between his teeth, and asks me to marry him.'

'And you,' grunts Mark, still struggling with the cork, 'said let me get back to you on that, haven't had my carbonara yet.'

'No,' goes Mum, laughing. 'I said yes, straight away.'

Pop. A champagne cork ricochets off the ceiling. And a lampshade. And one of my paintings.

'Woah,' shouts Mum, as though it's November the fifth and the sky is filled with colour.

The champagne is desperate to escape and starts gushing down the side of the bottle. Mark fills the glasses.

Way too quickly. Mostly bubble. We clink glasses and sip our froth.

Mum and Mark collapse onto the sofa, beaming like a couple of Lottery winners, without the giant cheque.

'Going to be such a belter of a day,' says Mark, staring at his new fiancée, as he grips her hand.

'And we'd like you to play a part too,' says Mum, her eyes going first to me, then to Lyin'.

My knee begins to bounce.

'We've been talking about the service. Mark and I thought it would be great for each of you to do a reading.'

Reprcssiouens

Tommy looks like he's been smacked in the face by a wrecking ball.

Too stunned to speak.

A reading.

In front of tons of people.

Naomi must have no idea how bad he is. Or, maybe, in all the excitement, she forgot.

'I'd love to do it,' I say, filling a hole the silence has dug.

'What about you, Tommy?' says Dad, smiling at him.

You'd think Tommy had been asked to sign his own death warrant.

'Sure,' he says, downing a glass he doesn't realise is already empty.

Reckon the last thing on earth Tommy wants right now is to read out loud at his mam's wedding.

'Don't mind doing both,' I say.

'I'll do it,' snaps Tommy, in a voice crackling with anger.

Dad and Naomi can sense a rip tide running through the room, threatening to drag us somewhere dangerous.

'Okay, well that's marvellous,' she says, raising her glass. 'I'm sure you'll both do an amazing job.'

One of us will.

Can tell the news has cast a dark cloud over Tommy. He grabs the champagne bottle from the coffee table, refills his glass and drains it.

Need to be alone. Not because of Tommy, but someone who's not here.

'Dad, going upstairs to do some history.'

'Stay a bit longer.'

'Got loads to do.'

'There's simply no stopping you, Ryan Dyer,' says Naomi, flushed with excitement. She gets up and gives me another hug.

Hurry upstairs to me room. Close the door and adopt the Tommy position, lying on me bed, staring at the ceiling.

Tears.

Funny how water can be so soft, yet feel so sharp.

They're tears of joy.

For Dad.

Never seen him so happy. Even on that summer holiday in Portugal, when everything seemed to go right. They were content then. Very content. Although they never quite made it to ecstatic. Which is where he is now.

For Naomi.

Can't have been easy for her. On her own all those years, trying to bring her son up the right way. And then he goes and chooses the wrong way. Now she's got someone else to focus on. A new husband. A new life.

They're tears of sadness.

For Mam.

Wonder what her reaction will be. Wonder if she knows. Check me phone. There's a missed call from her. Dad wouldn't have told her before us, would he? She's not gonna be happy about this. It doesn't take much to set her off nowadays. What am I going to say to her?

For me.

This really is the end. Until twenty minutes ago there was still a chance Dad and Naomi could split up, and Dad could get back together with Mam. It was a piece of straw so flimsy a normal drowning person would ignore it. But not me. When times were bad, I used to grab for it with flailing fingers. Now the piece of straw has finally drifted away. I can't reach it. It's officially gone.

They're tears of anger.

For being so selfish. For wanting something I couldn't have. For putting me happiness above theirs. Mam and Dad have fallen apart. It's not my job to glue them back together, to try to fix the unfixable.

They're tears of disappointment.

I want Tommy to like me. But since the crash he's only got room for hatred. The marriage means Tommy and I will be together, for ever. Even if he moves away, he'll come home to see his mam, for birthdays, Mother's Day, Easter, holidays, Christmas. He's going to be part of me life, whether he likes it or not.

Wipe me eyes.

Get a grip.

Think of the positives, Ryan, as they tell you to do in mindfulness sessions at school.

Positive one. Dad and Naomi have forgiven me for crashing the car.

Positive two. There are a million dating apps. Must be a guy for Mam in one of them.

Positive three. I...

Knock. Knock.

Wipe me eyes on me sleeve.

'Come in.'

The door opens.

Tommy.

This day is full to bursting with surprises. Although me room is only five metres from his, he hasn't been near it since that fateful Sunday. As if it's booby-trapped. Sit up on me bed. Tommy closes the door and walks to the window.

Try to read his expression. Can't.

Then he says the last thing I ever expected to hear.

'I want you to teach me to read.'

Rdeaing

Not sure I'd have got those words out without the champagne. I finished off the bottle, while the two love birds were busy cooing at each other. Wish Mum had just left it at the engagement. Why did she have to add the other bit?

It would be great for each of you to do a reading.

Simple enough request. Unless your number-one fear happens to be reading out loud to a room full of people. This won't be just any room, it'll be a church, packed with friends, relatives, strangers, all staring at me. And the icing on the cake: each mistake will be filmed on phones, cameras, for everyone to watch on repeat.

Play that bit again. Where he says the words backwards.

Could have found a way out of it. I'd got good at that. But for once, I didn't want to. All I've given Mum is grief. Now I need to make her happy, make her proud. If I pulled out, I'd have to sit there, listening to Lyin' Ryan's reading, as he grins like some smug Oscar winner.

Wasn't Mark's boy good?

Yeah, brilliant.

Should have got Mum to help me years ago. But, of course, Tommy Cavendish isn't wired that way. Wanted to keep it secret. For life. The way some people do. But it's pushing harder than ever to escape. I'm too ashamed to have to admit to it. If I do, I'll have to deal with Mum getting upset for not telling her, and for not realising how bad I really am. I can't have her wedding as the moment to reveal to the world what's been going on with me.

And the irony of it all, the person who can help me is the person I've been trying to avoid.

'You really want me to teach you?' says Lyin', his jaw dropping.

Yes, I do. I've never liked to ask for help. Only weak people do that. But I realise sometimes it's the only way.

'Didn't walk here for the exercise.'

'I, I thought you didn't want anything to do with me?' says Lyin', looking nervous.

'I didn't. Until Mum asked me to read at her wedding.'

He takes off his glasses and rubs his eyes. I probably don't look quite so scary when I'm blurred.

'Yeah, I'll do what I can.'

'You'll do better than that.'

Puts his glasses back. 'I'm not a teacher, Tommy.'

'No, but you're smart. You're dyslexic. Or so you say. You've been taught to read and write. Your room is six steps from mine. What more could I want?'

'What about the crash?' he asks.

I've got to be big enough to get over it. We both made stupid mistakes. Even though his was far stupider than mine.

'Let's forget about it, shall we?'

A big grin splits his face.

'Thanks, Tommy.'

'Don't get over-excited. You've got work to do.'

Hyclaiffe Prmairy Scoohl

A place I never really think about.

But I'm thinking about it today.

Haycliffe Primary School.

It delivers a satchel-full of memories. The fight with Dylan Marshall in Year Five. The time I wet meself in English. Trying to play keyboards at the Summer Fair when the sheet music blew off me stand. Being sick during PE. The performance of *Lion King* when I fell off stage and cut me head open. All the times Mam walked me here. Until I got too big to be walked.

I stare nervously at me phone.

What if she's no longer there?

Pull yourself together, Ryan.

Press the number with me thumb.

Ring. Ring.

'Morning, Haycliffe Primary School, how can I help yous?' says a woman with an accent that's all too familiar.

'Hi, I was hoping to speak to Mrs Hollings.'

'What's it aboot?'

A guy I live with has dyslexia but is too stubborn to admit it and he's been asked to read at his mam's wedding and has had a total meltdown so I thought I'd get some advice.

'It's a private matter. Private and urgent.'

'I think she's supervising the breakfast club, pet. Can I take your details and get her to call yous?'

'Aye, that would be great.'

Give her me details and hang up.

It's 7.40 a.m. She'd better call soon. Need to leave for school in half an hour. I pace up and down me miniature bedroom, hoping she's got the message, and praying she does something about it.

Ten minutes later me prayers are answered.

'Hello.'

'Hi, is that Ryan?' says Mrs Hollings in a cheery voice.

'Aye.'

'What a surprise. Must say, I was intrigued when I got the message private and urgent. Don't get many of them.'

She laughs.

I laugh too. To keep her company.

'So where are you now?'

'Down in London.'

'Enjoying school?'

'Sometimes.'

'How are your mam and dad?'

'Divorced.'

'Oh, I am sorry. Hopefully it's been amicable.'

'Not really.'

'Well, let's get on to the business of the day.'

'I have a question.'

'Fire away.'

'It's about dyslexia.'

'How are things in that department?' she asks.

'They're fine, Mrs Hollings. Reading and writing all good. I'm looking mostly at predicted grade nines and eights.'

'Wow, so why are you asking about it?'

'Thing is, I need to teach someone with dyslexia. Help them read. Especially out loud.'

'You're not qualified to do that, Ryan.'

'I know. But it's for a friend.'

'How old are they?'

'Seventeen.'

'They should ask the school.'

Mrs Hollings has never met Tommy.

'It's not that easy.'

Think I hear a sigh. I'm eating into her valuable prep time. But I reckon Mrs Hollings is the sort who's too nice to ignore me request.

'Well, to start with you need to assess the level of dyslexia. As you know, it can vary hugely from one person to the next. There are seven different types – phonological, surface, visual, primary, secondary, double deficit and acquired dyslexia.'

I take me pen and begin to make notes.

'The best thing, Ryan, is to have a proper assessment by a specialist teacher or educational psychologist.'

'Not a schoolboy?'

'Definitely not.'

'What would you recommend?'

'If it was me, I'd make sure they had an eye test and, ideally, a hearing test. I'd get them to bring in examples of schoolwork. It might be a book they're reading, or some written work. It's a good idea to get them to read out loud. This will help you understand what level they're at.'

'Then what?'

Sense another sigh brewing in Mrs Hollings. But she holds it back.

'You look at what works and what doesn't work for that person. See their strengths and weaknesses and areas that need working on.'

'Then what?'

'You look into a learning strategy tailored to that person.'

'Like what?'

'You've heard of the Orton-Gillingham?'

'Vaguely.'

'They were the American pioneers who developed the idea of breaking down reading and spelling into bite-sized chunks, using letters and sounds. You could find their books in the library.'

'Aye.'

'And look at some of the things we did together to help you. Learning to touch type is brilliant. Get them to listen to audio books and read along with the recording. Break up reading and other tasks into more manageable periods. Make sure they ask for extra help from a teacher.'

Not sure Tommy's gonna buy the last one.

'What if reading is their big problem?'

'You need to stop your friend from guessing words. They could try revealing words slowly with their finger, building up the word syllable by syllable.'

Like Na-o-mi.

'Some people suggest using a coloured overlay, or dyslexia friendly fonts. And build a bank of recognised and understood words.'

'How long will it take?'

'How long's a piece of string, Ryan? Everyone's different. It's much easier with young children.'

'What about seventeen-year-olds?'

'It can be done. But it may take a bit longer.'

'Thanks, miss,' I say, suddenly feeling like a primary-school kid again.

'Well, I hope that's been of some help, Ryan. It's been lovely talking to you. And I hope your friend sees an improvement in their reading.'

'Yeah.'

'Bye, Ryan.'

'Bye, Mrs. Hollings.'

I hang up.

Why on earth did I agree to all this?

The qstieouns

The road sign says 20 per cent. Think this stands for gradient. But it could mean you have only a 20 per cent chance of making it to the top. Or 20 per cent of people die on this slope. The hill is an absolute killer. Even though I'm in a granny gear, I hardly seem to be making any headway on the bike.

'Bit of a thigh burner,' groans Mark, through gritted teeth.

More like a full body-burner. Every bit of me is on fire. Not that I'll tell him that. Don't want him to think I'm a quitter. Want him to know his fiancée's son is every bit as tough as he is.

'Only a few hundred metres to go,' he puffs.

I try everything to beat the hill, getting out of the saddle, weaving up the slope as Mark suggested, increasing my cadence. None of it makes much difference, the tarmac barely moving beneath my tyres. And still the hill goes on, my heart hitting me as hard as it can for agreeing to the stupid ride.

Finally look up and instead of road filling my field of vision, I see sky. We're nearly at the top. I press down on the pedals with all my weight, trying to blank out the pain. The pressure on my legs eases. The hill releases me. I'm free.

I find enough speed to unclip and stop by the side of the road. I bend over the handlebars, sucking in as much oxygen as I can. A large hand pats me on the back.

'Well done, Tommy. Top effort.'

I've been on a few rides with Mark now. He lends me his spare bike, and a pair of his cycling shoes, which luckily fit me perfectly. I'm more into team sports, but Mum and Mark are always on at me to go out.

A few miles along the road we find a café where every wall, fence, tree and bush has a bike leaning against it. Inside, the place is wall-to-wall lycra, ruddy-faced men and women, taking a well-earned breather. I grab a couple of seats while Mark goes to the counter. He comes back with cappuccinos and two enormous slabs of carrot cake.

'Here you go, Tommy. You've earned your scran,' he says, putting the tray down.

'Cheers.'

We sip our coffee and wipe away froth moustaches.

'I'm proud of you,' he says.

'For getting up that hill?'

'No, for being you.'

Weird thing to say. But let it pass. He settles into his chair, his thinking face on. 'How are things between you and Ryan?'

'Better.'

I've dropped the Lyin' and given him his old name back. Not that he'll ever know.

'I'm glad. We all need to move on.'

Must have been hard for Mark. His goody-two-shoes son getting into trouble, when he's the one meant to be looking after him. Bet Ryan's mum gave his ears a right battering over that. Then paying all that money for an accident he had nothing to do with. Partially caused by a guy he's got nothing to do with.

I'm almost tempted to tell him the real reason Ryan and I have signed a peace treaty, but the temptation quickly passes.

Mark wipes crumbs from his lips and takes a slurp of coffee. 'You okay about me marrying your mam?'

'Nothing to do with me.'

'It's got everything to do with you.'

Thought we were gonna stop to talk about football or something.

'I want you to be okay with it.'

'Yeah, I'm okay with it.'

He takes off his cycling gloves and looks at me. For longer than guys normally do.

'It must feel strange, living so long with just you and your mam, and then along comes me and Ryan.'

'I guess. But if you make her happy, you make me happy.'

Mark smiles, pleased with my answer. Not sure he'll be happy with my question.

'Why did you get divorced?'

Puts his cup down before it has a chance to reach his mouth.

'That's a big one.'

It is. But I need to ask it. I hardly know you, Mark Dyer, and you're about to marry my mum. If you've been divorced once, you might get a taste for it and do it again. Don't want her getting hurt.

He scratches the stubble on his chin. 'Katie, Ryan's mam, and I had a good relationship. At the start. But I guess over time, things began to go wrong. She lost her job. And with it, her confidence.'

'So the problems were all hers?'

'Didn't say that.'

Bet he wishes he'd never brought the subject up.

'Maybe I wasn't as supportive as I could have been. I was mad busy at work. We never used to row. Then we started rowing about everything. Things just fell apart.'

'Did you try and put them back together?'

'Course we did. We made a go of it... tried to make a go of it.'

'Did you go to counselling?'

'No.'

'Did you cut down on your work?'

'No.'

Sounds a bit half-hearted to me. If I'd been married to Alice, I'd have tried anything to keep her.

'Do you still like her?'

Mark blows coffee breath in my direction. 'Yeah, I still like her. She has her good qualities. But I don't love her anymore.'

'When did you leave her?'

'About two years ago. Then I met your mam.'

'How did you meet?'

Mum told me her answer. Want to hear his.

'Wow, and I thought that hill was tough.' Mark takes a sip of coffee. 'After Katie and I split, I wanted a fresh start. Found a job down in London that ticked all the boxes. But I was lonely. Didn't know many people down here. Downloaded a dating app. First person I met was your mam. Went to a bar. Hit it off. Arranged to meet again. Snowballed from there.'

Mum never mentioned an app.

'I know why you're asking me these things, Tommy. I left Ryan's mam because we no longer got on. But I love Naomi with all my heart. I'm never going to leave her. Everything's going to be fine, Tommy. Trust me.'

The last person to say that to me, is now serving eighteen months in prison.

Tsteing

Been thinking about what Mrs Hollings said.

Make that, worrying about what Mrs Hollings said. It seems so easy the way she talks about it. But I know it's not going to be. If only it was like playing the piano. Here are the keys. Here's the sheet music. Here are your fingers. Now get on with it.

What if Tommy has an extreme form of dyslexia that takes years to deal with? Years we don't have. What if he throws another Tommy tantrum and refuses to listen? What if I fail to help him read properly? I console meself with the fact that all I have to do is get him through one simple reading. Surely it can't be that difficult.

Time to pay Tommy a visit. I grab the things I need and head to his room.

'Morning, Mr Dyer,' he says, in his best pupil voice.

'Morning, Tommy.'

I sit down on his bed. He's sitting at his desk, books all over the place. I wipe me glasses on me T-shirt.

'Been doing some research into dyslexia and there are

a couple of things I must do. First, need to check your eyesight.'

'What for?'

'Because that's what the specialist teacher said.'

'Not got time to go to the optician.'

'Don't worry, I'll do it here,' I say, as I take out a page from the Sunday papers.

'What the hell's that?' goes Tommy.

'Me eye chart.'

I'd Googled the correct distance between letters and eyes and found it was six metres, or twenty feet. Not sure if me feet are a foot, but they're the only measuring tool I've got. I go over to Tommy and, placing one foot in front of the other, pace across his room. Only get to eighteen. Not ideal, but it'll have to do. I stick the paper to the back of his bedroom door.

'This is so dumb,' sighs Tommy.

'Now cover one eye and read as far down the paper, sorry chart, as you can.'

He puts a hand over one eye. 'Minsters wants rabbit action on tax.'

'It's Minister. And rapid.'

'Minister wants rapid action on tax,' he repeats. 'This is the worst opticians' in the world.'

'Keep reading.'

The sub-heading is in smaller type. Tommy reads slowly. Not sure if it's his eyesight, or his dyslexia.

'Problem for PM as Ministers attach his plans.'

'It's attack.'

'Close enough.'

'Keep going,' I say, pointing to another part of the paper. 'Read that bit of type on the right in red.'

'Ten holidays to Germany to be won,' says Tommy.

It actually says Guernsey, but seeing as Tommy can read the other words, I guess his eyes aren't the issue.

'Okay, now let's test your hearing.'

'I don't read with my ears.'

'I need to check your hearing, okay? I've got some objects to drop. Turn your head and face outside. I want you to tell me if you can hear a sound.'

Tommy sits on his chair, facing away from me, shaking his head. I look inside my plastic bag, take out one of Dad's tennis balls, and drop it on to the wooden floor.

'Ball.'

'You don't need to say what it is. Just raise your hand if you hear it or not.'

Tommy raises his hand.

I drop one of Dad's plastic bike locks.

Tommy's hand goes up.

I then drop other objects, in diminishing order of noise. A book, a fork, a pen, a rubber, a paper clip, and finally an elastic band. Tommy's hand goes up the instant they hit the floor, apart from the elastic band, which makes no sound whatsoever.

'Don't think there's a whole lot wrong with your hearing,' I say.

'Great. I'm cured.'

I sit down and take out a pen and paper from my plastic bag. 'Have a few questions. Can you tell me how your dyslexia manifests itself?'

'It manifests itself when I come across words like manifest. In fact, it could be any word.' Tommy folds his arms across his chest. 'It's like my eyes and my brain have stopped talking to each other. My eyes see one thing, my brain sees another, as if it doesn't agree with what's been written.'

'Like what?'

He pulls a face as he tries to explain the inexplicable. 'If there are unusual words, names or places, my brain struggles to fathom out what they are. Like saying minster instead of minister. They're little traps. They catch me when I least expect it.'

'What do you do when you come across words like this?' I say.

'Ignore them. Or make something up. Depends how stressed I'm feeling.'

Tommy's right knee is starting to bounce. He's finding it hard to talk about this. Tommy, the cool kid. The babe magnet. The dyslexic.

'I can forget words from one page to the next, even though I've just read it. I might miss words out or add words that aren't even there. I do weird stuff all the time.'

This could be the worst wedding reading ever.

'Were you like that?' he says, turning to me.

'Yeah,' I say, even though I don't think I struggled that much. Remember teachers telling me mam me reading and writing weren't too clever. Mrs Hollings stepped in and a few months later I'd caught up with most of the other kids.

'And it's worse when you have to read out loud?'

'Million times. And when there's a crowd there, *bam*, nothing works. Like my dyslexia has spread to the rest of my body. Get sweaty. Heart goes insane. Mouth dries up. Can't breathe. Like I'm falling apart.'

'A sort of panic attack?'

'I guess.'

Got taught in school about the fight-or-flight mechanism hard-wired into every human. The adrenalin we needed to run away from prehistoric animals, now makes Tommy run away from words.

'Do you always feel anxious?'

'Only when I'm going to make a fool of myself. So pretty much all the time.'

Can tell Tommy's finding this hard, but the good news is he's talking. Like when you go to the doctors. You've got to tell them stuff, no matter how embarrassing. Or you might die.

'You gonna be able to sort it, aren't you?' he says, eyeballing me.

My fingers fiddle with the corner of his duvet. 'I'll try.'

'I need a lot more than try. I need you to fix this,' he says, his voice growing louder. 'I'm not gonna let her down. You are not gonna let me down. You owe me, Ryan. Big time.'

Ephaelnt

Not sure about my new teacher.

All that stuff with the eye chart and the hearing test. Not even convinced he is dyslexic, what with his top grades in everything. Could be trying to get sympathy, pretending we've got something in common, when we have nothing. Wouldn't put it past him. But he offered to help. Why would he do that if he didn't know about it? If he's lying, I really will end up back in Feltham.

Ryan got me to do some reading out loud to see how bad things were. He chose a piece with long words and unusual names in it. It didn't go well. Said I need to practise to improve my fluency and boost my confidence. Also said I need help with phonemic awareness. Think he read that bit online. Said phonemes are the smallest units of sound in the English language, such as 't' and 'e'. People like me struggle with recognising which sound goes with which letter, how many sounds there are in a word, and knowing which order they come in.

He told me I should learn to touch type, like him. Said

it will help with coursework, and allow me to check my spelling on spellcheck. Gave me a few free online courses I could use. He's also given me online exercises to do and told me to download teaching apps. Some of them seem babyish. Lots of cartoon pictures of animals. I need to try and break up the words in my head, then put them together like Lego. Already been put back one year at school. Feel like I've been put back ten more.

Don't want anyone knowing what I'm up to, so I practise the words in my head, only saying them out loud when I'm sure nobody's near. The journey to school is a good time to do this. Ryan says it's probably best if I practise on my own, so we sit at different parts of the bus, him at the front, me at the back. Just like at school.

We catch the bus. I grab a seat near the back, find the app.

'Ele-phant,' I say quietly to myself, as I look at a picture of an elephant's trunk called 'Ele' and the rest of his body called 'phant.'

'Bit old to be looking at cartoons, aren't you, Tom Cat.'

Damn.

Turn around to see two beefy lads, Craig and Harry, from my old school, leering over the seat at me. Was so caught up in my phone, didn't even see them get on. Before I have a chance to turn it off, Craig grabs it from me.

'Well, look at this,' he laughs, 'a learn-to-read app.'

Behind Craig and Harry sit a couple of girls I vaguely recognise. The app is a big source of amusement. They're all laughing. Guess they don't get much entertainment on the bus.

'Someone in prison steal your books?' says Harry.

'Stole his brain more like it,' goes Craig.

'Give it back,' I say, trying not to sound desperate.

'I'll give it on one condition. You can spell diarrhoea.'

More laughs from the girls.

Want to smack Craig's teeth down his throat, but I know one wrong move and I can kiss goodbye to Mum's wedding. I'm not gonna sit quietly and let him humiliate me. Need to do something. Then I spot it, a scuffed black shoe, sticking out from under my seat. I stand up, digging my heel into his foot, putting every bit of my weight on to it.

'Aggh,' he screams.

'What's the matter? Not even touching you.'

'Aggh,' he shouts again. 'You're on my bloody foot.'

'I'm standing up. That's all.'

Press down harder with my heel. Craig passes me the phone. I plunge it deep into my pocket and sit down.

'You bastard,' he shouts.

I turn to glare at Craig. 'If you must know, I'm checking out apps for my six-year-old niece, who has dyslexia.'

'Why didn't you say so?' says Craig, grimacing as he rubs his foot.

I settle into my seat, heart battering away inside my blazer.

'You asked me to spell diarrhoea. U-R-A-S-H-I-T.'

And this time the girls laugh at him.

Mma's paln

Been avoiding her.

Six missed calls. Got enough on my plate with me GCSEs and Tommy. But I can't ignore her for ever. She's me mam.

Find her in me phone. A little circle with her smiling face in it. Wonder what sort of face I'll see when I call her? The twisted one, contorted by the pain me dad's caused her? The sad one, for the life she no longer has?

I summon me courage and press her number. She appears almost instantly.

'Hello, gorgeous boy.'

Seems in a surprisingly good mood. But I know her good moods are like rainbows. They never last long.

'Hi, Mam.'

'Been ignoring me?'

'Na. Been busy.'

'Deein' what?'

'Studying.'

'So your dad and her are getting married,' she says, through lips clamped so tight I'm amazed her words can find a way out.

'Aye.'

'What do you think about that, then?'

Careful, Ryan.

'I hope it works. For them.'

Mam leans closer to the phone, as if letting me in on a secret. 'Do you know how long it took your dad to ask me to marry him? Three years. Three whole years. He's known this woman barely a year.'

Sounds like a maths question. Mark married Katie after three years. He married Naomi after one year. As a percentage, how much longer had Mark known Katie than Naomi?

'Sorry,' I say, without knowing what I'm saying sorry for.

'He's the one should be saying sorry. Talk about on the rebound.' Mam sits back in her chair. 'Suppose they're gonna have a big church wedding. All the bells and whistles. We had a registry office with thirty people. Are they having a big wedding, Ry?'

'Dunno.'

'Can you find out, please? And her wedding dress. Their honeymoon. I want to know everything. And pictures. If you've got pictures of anything, I want to see them too.'

Last thing I'm going to do. But sometimes it's easier to agree. Then say you forgot.

'Sure.'

'Next thing I know they'll be buying a house together.'

Dad's obviously kept that under wraps for another day. Should I tell her? Might as well.

'Mam, they've already bought a place.'

She slaps a hand to her cheek. 'I shoulda known it. What's it like?'

'Four walls, a roof, windows. The usual.'

Can tell from her face I'm not giving her what she wants.

'Do you like it, Ry?'

'Not much,' I say, because that's what she wants to hear.

'Not like our old place, eh?'

'Still, now that's sold you can buy somewhere nice of your own,' I say, enthusiastically.

'There wasn't that much left, Ry. We had a big mortgage. Is it bigger than our old house?'

'No, much smaller.'

'Can you send me some photos?'

Want to tell her to stop. Get her own life. But I don't. I never do. The words are there. But they remain unused.

'Yeah, I'll get some shots.'

'Bet your dad's cockahoop. New wife. New house. He'll be having kids next.'

The thought of sharing a house with Tommy and a baby is too weird to comprehend.

'What's the Feltham felon been up to?'

Come on, Ryan. Man up. Boy up.

'Please don't call him that.'

Tommy is nowhere near as bad as Mam wants him to be.

'He's your besty now, is he?'

'I'm just saying he's... okay.'

Mam runs her fingers through her hair. 'Okay? My, they've done a good job brainwashing you. Tommy was part of a gang that got jailed for a combined total of eight years. You're saying people like that are okay?'

'Yeah, you're right. Probably evil through and through.'

'Don't go all sarcastic with me, Ryan Dyer.'

I'm a millimetre away from ending this call.

Mam calms herself with some inhalations. 'I just want what's best for you, Ry. And you're not going to get it where you are now. That's why I've come up with a plan.'

Me heart sinks.

'What is it?'

'Is your passport up to date?'

'Passport? What do I need that for?'

'We're going to America.'

No scapeing hte psat

Been taking a different route to school. Not that I'm scared of lads like Craig and Harry. I just need to stay out of trouble. Unfortunately, it has a habit of finding me, no matter how hard I try.

'Tommy Cavendish?'

'Yeah?'

'Carter Hopkins.'

Recognise the blazer, not the name. The guy's from a secondary school on the other side of town. Carter's a bit taller than me, but what he's got in height, he lacks in width. Seen more fat on a chip. I know too well it isn't muscle that counts, it's the anger you have. And Carter's eyes are telling me he has anger to spare.

'You and me need to talk.'

'Why?' I say, folding my arms, defiantly.

'Want a quiet word. Come with me.'

Feltham didn't teach me much, but what I did learn was that sizing up people is a key survival skill. This guy smells of danger.

'We stay out here, in the open.'

I check for CCTV cameras. They're everywhere nowadays. Apart from this street. There are a few people about. Unlikely he'd try anything stupid. But you never know.

'Okay, have it your way,' he says, cracking his knuckles.

We walk to the edge of the pavement. A group of girls go past with their heads down, worshipping their phones. I wait until they've gone.

'What's your problem, Carter?'

'You are.'

I do what my brain's pleading with me not to do. Take a step towards him. Need to let him think I'm not scared.

'And why might that be?'

Carter's knuckle cracking goes up another level.

'You stitched up my cousin. You stitched up Logan.'

Hadn't heard his name for a while, but, like an echo, knew it would be back sooner or later.

'And what makes you think that?' I say, trying to keep my voice steady.

'To get a reduced sentence.'

I laugh.

'Won't be doing that when Logan gets out.'

Knew this day was coming. But I'm ready for it.

'You couldn't be further from the truth.'

'So what exactly is the truth, Tommy Cavendish?' says Carter, glaring at me.

'Heard of Section 49, the Regulation of Investigatory Powers Act?'

Carter shakes his head.

Neither had I until I Googled it.

'It gives the police powers to demand access to your phone password.'

'Which you refused?'

'Under Section 53, refusing is a criminal offence, which can add two years to your sentence. My solicitor told me I had to hand it over. I had no choice.'

Carter doesn't seem like the sharpest knife in the drawer. Can tell from his blank face he's never heard about any of this.

'Logan says you gave them your PIN.'

'Logan's wrong.'

When the police took me to the station and asked for access to my phone, I gave it to them without a second thought. They already had more than enough evidence to convict me. What I didn't know was my phone gave them all the evidence they needed to convict Logan and the others as well. They'd have found it all sooner or later, but I saved them the effort.

'I'd never do anything to help the cops. I'd never do anything to stitch up Logan. He's a mate.'

Can feel the anger subside in Carter. Confusion takes its place.

'How come you got a lighter sentence?'

'Had no previous convictions. And I wasn't the ringleader. I was a foot soldier. Don't blame me. Blame the British legal system.'

Hate having to explain myself to a lowlife like Carter. But if it can put a full stop to this, it'll be worth it.

'Why haven't you told Logan any of this?'

'Part of my licence. Not allowed to make contact with him or any of the other guys. Not even allowed in his postcode.'

Again, bending the truth. But he's not to know that.

'Got all the answers, haven't you?' says Carter, spitefully. 'Reckon Logan will still want to talk to you.'

'No, problemo. You know where to find me.'

Carter looks to the skies, as if trying to dredge up something smart, but Carter and smart clearly aren't on speaking terms. He walks off, kicking leaves as he goes.

I breathe out the air bottled inside me.

Hope to God he believes all the bull I've just told him.

Hte brthadiy crad

Can't get America out of me head.

It's way too big.

Know Dad will try and stop her. But Mam will be prepared. She'll go to court and say he's a bad parent. That he failed to reveal her son would be living with an ex-criminal. Mam will reveal exhibit A, a photo of me with a broken arm. Then exhibit B, a photo of two smashed cars in a car park. She'll say Tommy was responsible for both. The court will find in her favour.

Custody of Ryan Dyer granted to his mother.

This is all I need right now.

The door opens. Tommy. He looks like the version I see in English lessons. Awkward, fidgety, embarrassed.

'What's up?'

'Got a favour to ask,' he says. 'Written a birthday card for someone. Like you to check the spelling.'

'Sure.'

He hands me a piece of handwritten paper from inside the card.

'Who's Sprout?'

'An ex-girlfriend. Her real name's Alice.'

'Why d'ya split up?'

'Seven letters. Starts with F and ends in m.'

'Why would you send a card to an ex?'

'Because I want to.'

I nod, as if I know about stuff like that. I went out with a lass once. It lasted four minutes and thirty-four seconds. That's how long 'I Will Always Love You' goes on for. It was the closing song at the school disco in Year Eight. It was the final time she spoke to me.

I take the paper and read what Tommy's written. Not an easy task.

'Have you started touch typing?'

Tommy shakes his head.

'It's a bit messy.'

'I'll sort that out later. All I want is for you to check the words,' he says, his voice notching up in volume. 'Sorry, but this sort of stuff stresses me out.'

'It's okay,' I say, going back to his words. 'Few mistakes. Not too many. And some punctuation errors.'

Tommy nods, as if he was expecting as much. 'I don't just struggle with words, struggle with those stupid little squiggles that come with them. Concentrating so much, I forget to add them.'

'Can sort that,' I say, grabbing a pen. 'Can I write on this?'

'Sure.'

I make the corrections.

'You haven't put your name.'

'That's one thing I do know how to spell.'

I read the final bit.

Ps hope you like the picture.

'Which picture?'

Tommy's awkwardness goes up a notch.

'Just something I drew.'

'Can I see it?'

'Nothing special.'

'Still like to see it.'

He hands me the card. It's a beautiful drawing of a girl with reddish hair, green eyes, and the faintest hint of a smile on her lips.

'Wow, she's amazing. You're amazing.'

'Okay, fan-club meeting over,' says Tommy, grabbing it back.

'I'm being honest, Tommy. You're really good. She's very pretty.'

'Looks even better in real life,' says Tommy, looking lovingly at the picture. 'She's eighteen next week.'

'Cool.'

Tommy stands there, staring longingly at her face.

'Better get back to me homework,' I say.

'What you doing?' he asks.

'Circle theorems.'

'Really? That book says *Guide to New York*.'

Tmmoy's Iceince

Promised myself I'd never go there again.

Another promise bites the dust.

The café's busier than I hoped. Every table taken. People catching up over steaming mugs and cakes. Young men and women in black scurrying about. Join the queue that stretches almost to the door. Spot Alice. She's behind the counter drawing little leaves on coffee froth.

Want to deliver the card by hand. But now I'm here, I wish I wasn't. She'll be too busy to talk. But maybe that's a good thing.

The gap between me and her narrows. I reach the front of the queue.

'Yeah?' grunts a surly young guy, not suited to the hospitality industry.

'Got something for Alice.'

He turns. 'Alice, this bloke has something for you.'

Alice turns. Her face is red. Can't tell if it's me, or the heat from the kitchen.

'Oh, Tommy,' she says, wiping her hands on a towel.

'Happy birthday for tomorrow,' I say, handing her the card.

'What you doing here?' booms a deep voice.

I turn. Her dad towers over me. His expression could best be described as disgust.

'Nothing. I'm just leaving.'

I hurry away past the long line of people queuing for their caffeine.

'Tommy,' shouts Alice.

But I'm not going back. Not ever.

Embarrassed Alice. Embarrassed me. Why didn't I post it?

Run home, race to my bedroom and slam the door. There's an old photo of Alice stuck to my wardrobe. It's a close-up of her, sitting on a bench by the river, wearing that blue T-shirt I bought her. She has her pre-Feltham face on, gazing at me with love, and a little bit of pride thrown in for good measure. Now someone else is on the receiving end of that look.

Next to the photo is the picture I drew of her. Decided it wasn't good enough for her card. What did Ryan say? Wow. But the picture is a million miles from wow. The hair is all wrong. The nose is crooked. Her mouth is too big. It's more like a cartoon. I grab the picture and tear it to pieces.

Alice lies in tatters on the floor. Her eyes look up at me, as if to say – *you're useless, Tommy. Can't even draw properly*.

Look at the one word written on my whiteboard – wedding. Another moment of humiliation awaiting me.

I wipe the word away with my hand. Reckon I've been thinking more about it than Mum does, and she bangs on about it every second of the day. Imagine myself being called up in front of all those people, dozens of eyes lasering in on me, dozens of ears waiting for a mistake. I have to nail that reading. Right now, it means more to me than my mocks. They're just a bunch of numbers. If they're good enough, they get you into Sixth Form, where you're given some letters. If they're good enough you can go to university where you go back to getting numbers again. Letters. Numbers. What difference does it make?

Not sure I want to keep studying. Read somewhere there are no jobs anyway. At least, not for people like me. Might as well leave the country. That would make everyone happy. The school. Logan. Logan's mates. Alice. Alice's dad. Their worlds would be so much better without me there.

'Tommy,' shouts Mum.

Now what?

'Mrs Brighton's here.'

A shiver finds me every time I hear that name. She has the power to ruin everything. Reluctantly, I make my way downstairs. Mum's waiting at the bottom, smiling at me.

'She's in the dining room.'

Mum grips my arm when I reach her, and whispers in my ear. 'You're not keeping anything from me, are you?'

She's like the others. Thinks I might do it again. Reckons the temptation will be too strong for me.

'I don't want any more secrets, Tommy.'

'I'm not hiding anything, Mum. I promise.'

She kisses me on the cheek. 'Better not keep her waiting.'

I open the door to the dining room. Mrs Brighton is sitting there with a mug of tea. *World's Best Mum* on its side. She has my case notes laid out on the table in front of her. She's dressed smart, like it's an interview. Which I guess it is.

'Hello, Tommy,' she says, cheerily.

Mrs Brighton is ever so smiley. Reckon she wears it to put people at ease. It puts me on edge.

'Hi, Mrs Brighton,' I say, sitting opposite her.

Most of my meetings are at her office. But sometimes she comes to my house, to check everything is okay.

'How's it going, Tommy?'

'Good.'

She makes notes. Can tell she's written a lot more than the word 'good'. But a combination of dyslexia, scrawly writing, and the words being upside down make it impossible to tell what.

'Your mum tells me she's marrying Ryan's dad.'

'Yeah.'

'How do you feel about that?'

'Happy. For Mum.'

'What about you?'

'Yeah, guess I'm happy too.'

Apart from the humiliation heading my way.

'Do you get on with your Mum's fiancée?'

'Yeah. Seems okay.'

She makes more indecipherable notes.

'How's school going?'

'Okay.'

'And your mum's partner's son, Ryan. All good?'

'Yeah.'

'Got your GCSEs next year. Studying hard?'

'Yeah.'

She always starts this way. Questions you can swat away like flies. But I know the big one is coming. It always comes. She lowers her pen and knits her fingers together, as if she's praying. 'What about the other gang members. Have you heard from them?'

Does she know? Look at her face. But it's blank.

I'm not meant to have any contact with them. It hasn't stopped them trying to contact me. If I tell her one of Logan's guys has been in touch, it will get back to them. Causing trouble for him. For me.

'Not heard a thing from anyone.'

She stares at me. A human lie-detector.

Even though it's cold in here, can feel my face glowing.

'You sure about that, Tommy?'

'Yeah.'

'Would you like to read your licence conditions again?' she says, pushing a form in my direction.

'No, thanks.'

'You look a bit worried, Tommy. Are you sure everything's fine?'

'Yeah, Mrs Brighton, everything's fine, absolutely fine.'

Mma's spurrise

Me thoughts are like desert sand, drifting aimlessly. Today they've gone a very long way, from our town, through the English countryside, across Wales, the Irish Sea, Ireland, and over the Atlantic to America. Can't get the place out of me head. Whenever I push it out, it somehow barges its way back in.

Got some books about New York from the library. Seems an amazing place to visit. But living there's different. Won't know anyone apart from Mam's other sister Clara and three cousins I've never met. And you can't just turn up, can you? You have to have a job and schools and accommodation sorted.

I stumble through lessons, skyscrapers poking their way through me thoughts. School finally comes to an end. Meet Tommy as we leave. Everyone's used to him now, but it doesn't stop some of the girls throwing him the sort of glance they never throw at me.

'What y'up to, Tommy?' says a girl whose outfit pushes the school dress code to the absolute max.

'Walking.'

'Cool.'

He ignores her, as he does with all the girls who block his path.

I'd love to be given the chance to ignore someone one day.

We carry on out of school.

'How's it going?' I ask.

'Feel better when I know what I'm doing at the wedding.'

Dad and Naomi still haven't chosen the readings.

'I've been learning about public speaking, and how to cope,' I say, enthusiastically.

'Good for you,' says Tommy.

'It's about fear versus excitement. You're frightened because it might go badly. But it's also exciting because it might go really well. Fear is just another form of excitement. Think of the reading as something exciting, and it can turn disaster into triumph.'

Tommy shrugs as though I've said the most boring thing ever.

We carry on up the street.

'Must be dyslexics in the police force as well,' says Tommy, looking at a patrol car.

On the bonnet, written in big letters, is – ECILOP.

I laugh, but it quickly dies in me throat. I come to a dead stop, as though I've walked into a wall.

'Don't look so shocked. I *am* your mam.'

'What you doing here?'

'Whatever happened to "lovely you to see you, Mam"? Here let me give me boy a big hug.'

Mam wraps me in her arms and kisses the top of me head. Wish she wouldn't do that, not within sight of school. She finally releases me.

'Mam, this is...' oh, my God, this is... Tommy Cavendish, the guy she wants out of me life. The guy she thinks is a master criminal.

'I knaa who he is,' she says, looking him up and down.

If looks could kill, Tommy would be certified dead.

'Hello, Mrs Dyer,' he says, smiling, cool as anything.

Mam continues to give him the death-stare.

Want her to like him. Need her to like him.

'Tommy's in the school first eleven for football.'

She could not look more unimpressed if I'd said he liked yodelling.

'Let's go,' she says.

'See you later, Ryan. Nice to meet you, Mrs Dyer,' he shouts.

But Mam isn't listening as she drags me away through the forest of blazers.

'Why didn't you tell me you were coming?'

She says nothing, as she leads me by the elbow up the street. We turn a corner and I spot her blue VW. She flicks the doors open.

Is this wise? What if she plans to drive me away somewhere, like the airport? But she can't. I haven't got me passport. Or a toothbrush. Or a clean pair of boxers.

I get in next to Mam. She sits, staring straight ahead, gripping the steering wheel tight, as though she's doing ninety.

'So that's the famous Tommy Cavendish.'

'He's not famous, Mam. He's just a guy.'

'Whatever.'

Had enough of this.

'Mam, are you ever going to stop this... hating?'

'When you've been lied to as much as I have, Ryan, it comes easy. You, of all people, know what I've been through. What you've been through. I can't sit by and do nothing. No mam in her right mind would do that.'

'But what's it going to achieve?'

Mam ignores me question. Think she knows it's gonna achieve nowt. Apart from revenge. She looks out through the windscreen, ignoring the parking ticket under the wipers. Wonder how long she's been waiting at the school gate.

Shrink into me seat. Pull the sun visor down. Don't want anyone from school seeing me.

'Spoke to your Aunty Clara. She thinks it's too soon to be coming over. Especially in your GCSE year. We'll wait until the summer, when you've done your exams. Give me a chance to plan everything.'

'Do I get a say in this?'

'I have a duty as your mam to do what's best for you. When you leave school you're free to do as you wish. But until then I need to protect you.'

'From what?'

'The situation you're in.'

'Mam, I'm okay with this situation. I like Naomi, and, believe it or not, I like Tommy.'

Mam looks as if she's been slapped. She sits there, breathing rapidly.

'My, they've done a good job on you.'

See a woman walking home with her son. Bet they're not having a conversation like ours. Why can't we talk about climate change, or what's on telly tonight?

'Feel as though I've hardly seen you,' she says. 'Apart from on that stupid little screen. That's why I've been thinking about Christmas. Thought it would be nice for you to spend the holidays with us.'

Me heart plummets.

'The whole holidays?'

'No, just a couple of minutes. Of course, the whole holidays. It will be lovely to have some time together. With your gran and grandad. They miss you like mad.'

'But what will I do?'

'We can go for walks.'

'I'm not a dog'.

'Any rate, you'll be studying for your mocks. Too busy to do much.'

Mam leans across and hugs me tight. For way too long. I used to love her hugging me. Now it feels different. Like she wants to own me.

'I'm gonna get you out of that house, Ryan, if it's the last thing I do.'

Ryn's prbloem

Hearing about six lads who go off the rails. A bit like my story, except these lads live on a desert island. It's called *Lord of the Flies.* Reached the bit where the sadistic Roger pushes a boulder down a cliff and kills Piggy, when my door opens. Ryan. He normally knocks. Maybe he did, but the sound was drowned out by Roger's giant rock. Pause the story. Try to read Ryan's face. It's telling me one thing. Something bad is going on in there.

'What's up, dude?'

Bet it's got something to do with his mam turning up outside school.

'Me mam.'

One-nil to Tommy.

'Is she okay?'

Ryan looks sad. 'Na, she's not. Talking about me and her gannin' to America next year, after me exams.'

'For a holiday?'

'No, for good.'

Explains the book on his desk.

'What's your dad say about that?'

'He doesn't know.'

'She's gonna kidnap you?'

'Reckon she'll go to court, get custody of me.'

'On what grounds?'

'Me dad. He didn't tell her he was moving me into a house with a guy who's been inside.'

'Why did he keep it a secret?'

'Cos she'd have said no, which would have ruined all his plans.'

Always thought I was missing out not having two parents. Now I look at Ryan I'm not so sure. Stuck in the middle of a conflict that goes on and on and on.

'What you gonna do?'

'Don't know,' says Ryan, wiping his glasses on his school tie. 'Should tell Dad, but I know he'll gan mad. Probably ban me from seeing her. I don't want that either. I'm fed up with all this.'

Ryan needs to play it cool for a while. But not sure he knows how.

'Does she know about the wedding?' I ask.

He nods.

'That's what this is all about. She's angry her ex has found happiness and she hasn't. Once the wedding's over she'll calm down. Believe me.'

Ryan's expression says – what do you know about stuff like this?

He gets up and walks to the door.

'Mam also wants me to go and spend Christmas with her in Coventry. All of it.'

'Not the end of the world.'

'I need to be here, helping you with your reading.'

'You can only do so much, Ryan. I'm the one who's gonna have to get up on stage, altar, whatever, and do it.'

Ryan looks like he wants to go. But something's stopping him.

'There's another reason I don't want to go stay with me mam.'

'What's that?'

'Wanna spend Christmas here, with you.'

Shksepeear

'Okay, Ryan?'

'Aye.'

Naomi pats the sofa next to her. I sit down, curious to know what she's after.

'I've got something for you. Your wedding reading.'

I force a smile. Know what a massive deal this is for her.

'Do you like Shakespeare?'

'He's okay.'

'Yeah, he wasn't bad. Well, here's a little sonnet he wrote.'

She opens her laptop, and hands it to me. There on the screen are my words.

Let me not to the marriage of true minds
Admit impediments. Love is not love
Which alters when it alteration finds,
Or bends with the remover to remove:
O no! it is an ever-fixed mark

That looks on tempests and is never shaken;
It is the star to every wandering bark,
Whose worth's unknown, although his
height be taken.
Love's not Time's fool, though rosy lips and cheeks
Within his bending sickle's compass come:
Love alters not with his brief hours and weeks,
But bears it out even to the edge of doom.
If this be error and upon me proved,
I never writ, nor no man ever loved.

Shakespeare, Sonnet 116

Can't imagine how Shakespeare found the time to write 116 of those, along with all his other stuff. Suppose he didn't have the internet, a mobile phone, or Netflix.

'Yeah, it's nice,' I say.

'Nice? It's flippin' gorgeous.'

'Yeah, that's what I meant.'

Naomi laughs. 'Thought I'd give you the reading early. Give you plenty of time to prepare.'

Don't think I need six weeks for that. Six minutes will do. Not sure I can say the same for her son.

'What about Tommy? Where's his reading?'

'Mark will give it to him. I'll print this off for you.'

'Thanks.'

'How are your studies going?'

'Good.'

'I know we've had a few bumps in the road, but wanted to say how proud I am of the way you've handled everything.'

It's horrible to have to say it, but I will anyway, Naomi's nicer than me mam right now. Not the old one, from way back, but the new one with the crazy ideas. Naomi's kind, friendly, not too bossy. Usually leaves it to Dad if I need telling off. She's never bitter, but I guess she's got nothing to be bitter about. Living with Tommy can't have been easy, but if it's been tough, it doesn't show. Bet she's never done a bad thing in her life.

And then her face goes serious, like doctors do in films when they've got bad news.

'How's your mam?'

Of all the questions.

'She's okay,' I lie.

'I assume she knows about the wedding?'

'Aye. And the new house.'

She sits there. Thinking.

Bet Naomi would love to ask more. But even if she did, I wouldn't say.

She leans over and wraps me up in her arms. It feels good. Even though they're not the right arms.

'Don't worry, Ryan. Once the wedding's over, and we're settled in our new place everything will be different.'

Aye, because not long after that I'll be four thousand miles away.

Faer

Want to move on. But I'm manacled to the past. Logan will be out of prison next year. He'll want revenge. Or for me to get involved in something stupid. I just know it. I'll say no. I have to say no. But what will the repercussions be? Mum says, 'a problem's not a problem until it's a problem.' Logan may not be one now, but he will be soon.

Then there's the problem that's always there, waiting for me, in every book, on every page. I've started learning to touch type. And I've been doing the lessons Ryan set me. They seem to be going okay, but the last place I want to see whether they've worked is the actual wedding. I can read out loud with just Ryan there, but what will I be like with two hundred eyes on me?

I'm on my beanbag, listening to an audiobook of *Animal Farm*, when Mark appears in his running gear, holding a piece of paper. Take off my headphones.

'What you listening to?' he says.

'Music.'

'We should go see a band sometime.'

If the sort of music I hear on his car radio is anything to go by, I'd rather go to a museum.

'Maybe.'

He stands there looking awkward, as he usually does when he appears in my room.

'Your mum and I have chosen our wedding readings. Want to see yours?'

'Sure.'

Mark hands me the paper, and I read.

Try to read.

'Yeah, neat,' I say.

'Wow, that was fast.'

That's because I didn't read it. My eyes flew over the page, like a stone skipping across water. Know there are words I don't get. But don't need him to know that.

'Do you like it?' he asks.

'Yeah, it's cool.'

'You can keep it.'

'Cheers.'

I fold the paper and post it into my jeans pocket. Don't want to talk about the reading. Not now. Not to him.

'How are the preparations going?' I ask.

'Pretty good, Tommy. Got the reception booked at the cricket club. Catering's sorted. Invitations have gone out. Just awaiting the hate mail from those not on the list.'

Ryan's mum will probably send a letter bomb.

'Going to be such a great day,' he says, bending down to give my arm a firm squeeze. 'Maybe we could go on another bike ride this weekend.'

'Got an away match. And loads of study to catch up on.'

'Sure.'

He stands there, as if he's got more to say, but doesn't know how to say it.

'See you later, Tommy.'

'Yeah.'

Mark goes off to get sweaty. I take the paper out of my pocket, unfold it, and go through it again, this time at my normal ambling pace. There are a few words that trip me up, but it seems okay. Reading inside my head is cheating, though. I need to try it at volume, with someone listening.

Head to Ryan's room.

'Can I try my reading out on you?'

'Aye,' he says, looking up from his laptop.

'Out on the street.'

'The street?'

'Yeah, don't want Mum hearing me practise.'

Ryan grabs his coat and we head out of the front door. I find a spot up the road with a small patch of green and pull the paper from my pocket.

'What's your reading?' asks Ryan, the cold air turning his words to smoke.

'"The Art of Marriage", by some bloke.'

'Well you're pretty good at art.'

Almost funny, Ryan.

Clear my throat. Like I will on the day. Inflate my lungs. Clutch the paper.

'A good marriage must be created.'

Ding de ding dong.

An ice-cream van drives past. Who the hell eats ice-cream in winter? I stop and wait for the tinny sound to fade away. Can feel my heart echoing through my body. And I've only got an audience of Ryan. Pull yourself together, Tommy. Look around one last time to make sure no one's within earshot.

I go through the poem.

Ryan claps. 'That was great, Tommy.' Even though I know it wasn't. 'You only stumbled in a few places. Think you changed the odd word. And the pace was a bit fast.'

'In other words, a pile of steaming cow pat.'

'Stop panicking. It's weeks till the wedding. You can go through it a million times before then. It'll be perfect.'

I know what Ryan says is true.

But if it's true, why do I feel so scared?

Teh worng raeding

'Better gan too slow than too fast,' I say, as we walk home.

'Better to get it over with as quickly as possible,' he replies, screwing up the paper and ramming it into the back pocket of his jeans.

Decide to try a few more things I've read about. I find Tommy's reading online and print it out in bold with a much bigger type size. It's so large it now runs to three pages. I buy a yellow overlay to help him see the words more clearly. I lend him a ruler to place beneath each sentence, so he doesn't lose his place. Heard it helps to try visualising things, so I ask him to illustrate the text.

He shows me the little drawings he's made in the margins.

'Wow.'

'You being sarcastic?'

'My wow is 100 per cent genuine.'

He's drawn the most amazing little pictures in pencil. Two hands, fingers interlaced. A couple leaning into one another. Two mouths about to merge. A man and woman using each other's shoulders as head rests.

'Do you think any of this will do any good?' asks Tommy.

'No idea. Let's find out.'

'We're going out again?'

'Yes, Tommy, we're going out again. I'd like you to go through it a few more times, breaking up the tricky words the way you've been taught, and see how you go.'

Thought Tommy would push back. But he doesn't.

It's dark outside. We find a different place, underneath a street light. Tommy's nerves have come too. He sits on a garden wall, his right leg jerking. Gets out his paper, puts his coloured overlay on top of the first page, places his ruler under the first line, and takes a large gulp of breath. I close me eyes and imagine I'm wearing a suit, tie, and sitting on a hard pew in a cold church.

He starts to read.

A moment later it's all over.

'That was brilliant, Tommy. In fact, if someone told me the person reading that is dyslexic, I wouldn't believe them.'

'Honest?'

'Honest.'

Tommy has nailed it. Gone are the stumbles over difficult words. Pauses have disappeared in the steady flow. He's neither too fast nor too slow. In fact, he's word perfect. I pat his shoulder.

Proud of him.

Proud of me.

We head back.

At home we're met by the smell of something spicy in the kitchen.

'Where've you two been?' asks Naomi.

'Church,' says Tommy.

Naomi folds her arms. 'Guys, I don't want to turn into the Secret Police, but I wouldn't mind a bit of honesty once in a while.'

'We went for a quick walk, Mum.'

Decide to build on Tommy's lie. 'Aye, our teachers say it's good to take a breather when you've been studying, refresh the brain.'

Naomi's eyes go from Tommy to me and back again. Hard to tell whether she believes a word.

Her arms finally unfold.

'I've got some news for you, Tommy,' she says. 'About that speech Mark gave you.'

'Yeah?' he says.

'Going to have to find you a new one.'

Tommy's fists tighten. 'What d'ya mean?'

'You know my friend Hayley? Well, she's getting married the week before us. Guess which reading she's chosen? "The Art of Marriage", by Wilfred A. Peterson.'

Teh dscieovry

I snap Ryan's ruler, cut up the overlay, and tear the reading into pieces smaller than dandruff. What a complete and utter waste of time.

'It's okay,' says Ryan.

'What exactly is okay about it? Been working on that for ages. Going through it over and over.'

'You'll get another one.'

'There's a thing called time, Ryan, and it's running out. Can't study and work on a new reading. What if the next one's long and complicated? Shakespeare, or Chancer.'

'Chaucer.'

'Yeah, him.'

Why couldn't Hayley have picked Ryan's reading?

'You can have mine,' he says.

'Don't want yours. It's weird, old words. Don't want to be in the spotlight. Don't want any of this.'

Ryan walks out of my room. Wouldn't blame him for giving up on me.

I was so up to speed on that reading. Knew it off by heart. Why did Mum have to go and change it? Most weddings are the same anyway. If Hayley picked a cake, would Mum go for a bowl of rice pudding? I was finally heading in the right direction, but my luck has done a handbrake turn, tyres squealing, dust flying.

I want to try and change Mum's mind. But if I do she'll know something is up.

Why are you making this such a big deal?

Because I'm scared of reading in public. Because I'm dyslexic.

As each day trickles by without her making her choice, it's another day less to prepare. Another day to worry. Mum begins to notice.

'You've been very quiet, Tommy?'

Because you stole my words.

'I'm...okay,' I say, in my least okay voice ever.

'Is it the money you owe for the car?'

'No.'

'Have you and Ryan fallen out again?'

'No.'

Ryan has been removed from my worry list. Since I asked for help, he's got totally into the whole teaching bit. Think he gets a buzz out of hearing me read properly. Takes his mind off other things. Like his mam. Or soon to be Mom.

Can almost hear the cogs in her head whirring as Mum searches for other reasons for my grumpiness.

'Is it your GCSEs?'

'No, Mum.'

But this could quickly turn into a yes. Still feel like I'm studying at half-speed compared to everyone else.

'If nothing's the matter, would you mind doing a small job for me?'

'What?'

'Can you go through your things in the loft? There's a ton of stuff we need to get rid of before we move.'

'But you said we're not moving until after the wedding.'

'It'll be here before you know it. Don't want to do everything last minute. And bring the Christmas decorations down. We'll need to put them up soon.'

'Yeah.'

'Thanks, Tommy.'

And she gives me one of her 'everything's going to be all right' hugs.

Don't fancy going into the loft, but it'll give me something to do. Go upstairs, grab a pole and open the hatch. Pull the metal ladder down and make my way up the steps. Scramble through the hole and search for the light. A flick illuminates the space. Haven't been up here for ages. A quick sweep of the loft tells me why. It's a mad jumble of boxes, papers, suitcases, old lamps, decorations, pictures, clothes, bags, and household junk. It's like the back room of a charity shop.

Hard to know where to begin. I could ask Ryan for help, but that wouldn't be fair. It's a mountain that's been built by Mum and me over the last seventeen years. None of it belongs to him.

Decide to leave the decorations till last. I stoop low under the beams, and make my way to the farthest corner, until I'm half-buried by the remnants of our lives. The first box I find is full of children's books. They look as if they've never been opened. Guess someone bought them for me for Christmas or my birthday. Imagine me ripping open the wrapping with little fingers, eyes popping, hoping for something exciting. Conjuring a fake smile when I see it's a book. Then dashing outside to play before they ask me to read and find I can't. Wonder why Mum kept them.

I move the box near the mouth of the loft to carry downstairs later. Ease my way back into the tip and find some plastic bags full of clothes. T-shirts, hoodies, trousers, jumpers. Hold them up against me. All way too small. Most have designer tags. Wonder how Mum found the money to buy them, and why she bothered. Never been into labels. The bags of clothes join the books, waiting for their new home.

I crawl deeper into the eaves, like an archaeologist, exploring *The Tomb of Naomi and Tommy Cavendish*. But instead of treasure, this place is full of rubbish. Don't know why Mum has kept half of it. Like the loft has become some kind of limbo. Too bad for the house. Not bad enough for the skip.

Find boxes and boxes of Halloween stuff. Mum loves that time of year. Even though I outgrew it years ago, it all comes out every October, and she covers the house in fake horror – skeletons, cobwebs, spiders, freaky faces. And she gets a ton of sweets in for the kids who come knocking. Think it's to make up for the fact it's just been the two of us.

Another box. It's stuff belonging to Mum. Open a plastic envelope and find a stack of pictures. Flick through them.

They're glossy, like magazine covers, showing Mum years ago, about the same age as me now. I know Mum was a teenager once, but it's hard to imagine. Here she is, young, bright eyed, long hair, laughing.

Go deeper. Find a framed degree from Nottingham University. 2:1 in Geography. Forgot she did that. Dive further. There's a blue folder buried at the bottom. Open it. It's full of letters. Know I shouldn't look at them, but I've suddenly got into this. And now my reading's getting better no harm in taking a peek at mum's past.

I take out a couple of the letters and move over to the light to read them. Handwriting I don't recognise.

My darling Naomi.

It's that feeling I get watching those sites you're not meant to look at. The ones everyone looks at. Know I shouldn't go further, but there's nobody here to catch me. Hold the worn paper in my hands. It gives me that buzz again. Like the one that started all the trouble.

The light isn't great, a 40-watt bulb in a 100-watt space, but it's good enough. Squint at the page. Some of the handwriting is hard to figure out, but I slowly unravel the words in front of me.

As I do my vision begins to blur.

My stomach begins to sink.

My world begins to crumble.

Mrrey Crsthmais

'Thanks, Mam, it's fantastic,' I mumble.

No.

'It's just what I always wanted.'

No.

'Wow, that's so sick.'

Definitely not.

I'm standing in front of the bathroom mirror, preparing me reaction for whatever it is Mam's got me for Christmas. As the situation between her and Dad worsened, so did the presents. Over the last few years I've had a music stand, a harmonica, a leather bookmark, a tuning fork, a mirror, the story of the Trans-Siberian Railway, and an owl paperweight. It's as though arguing destroyed their ability to shop.

I used to dash downstairs on Christmas morning. Today I move at tortoise speed. Open the sitting-room door. Mam, Gran and Grandad are sitting around a small fake tree, wearing silly hats.

'Merry Christmas, Ryan,' beams Mam.

'Merry Christmas, Mam.'

She gets to her feet and hugs me like she never wants to let go.

I kiss Gran and shake Grandad's hand.

'Santa's been,' says Gran.

I look down at an empty sherry glass, a silver foil where a mince pie once lived, and a half-eaten carrot.

'Breaking and entering again,' I mumble.

'That's why he's called Saint Nick,' says Grandad, earning him an elbow from Gran.

The opening ceremony begins. Presents and kisses are swapped. Boxes and packages are revealed. Then, in a matter of minutes, it's all over. For another year.

For once Mam's gone the extra mile. Maybe it's the money she got from the house. She's bought me a games console. A pair of Nike trainers. A leather belt. A new smart watch. And a sweatshirt with USA on the front. The last one also came with a secret wink. And I've still got presents from me dad and Naomi when I get home. Suppose being the son of divorced parents has to have some benefits.

Should have put a bit more effort into what I bought Mam. I got her a fancy box of toiletries, and four tins of tennis balls.

'You know I divvent play anymore?' she says.

'Sorry, I forgot.'

Her mixed-doubles partner used to be Dad.

'Maybe you can start again,' I say, hopefully.

'Maybe,' she mutters, putting the balls aside.

Feel guilty for having had such bad thoughts. Mam, Gran and Grandad have been dead generous.

'My, you've done well, lad,' says Gran, looking at me stash.

'Aye.'

'You deserve it, son,' says Gran, giving me yet another hug. Reckon she knows only too well what's gone on these last few months. The divorce was a tsunami that didn't just hit Mam, the waves washed right through their house too.

After sorting out me new watch, decide to go outside.

'Where you off to?' asks Mam, as I make for the kitchen door.

'Gonna call Josh.'

'Josh,' she says, putting extra volume behind his name so that it sounds like a rock dropped into a pond.

'Aye, him.'

Hurry into the back garden, pull out me phone and nervously press the number.

'What?'

And a merry Christmas to you too.

'Hi, Tommy, it's me, Ryan.'

'Course it's you, your name's on the phone. I can read *some* things, you know.'

Wow.

Deep breath, Ryan.

'How are things?'

'You know exactly how they are.'

Realise he's nervous about the wedding, but no need to take it out on me. I'm the person trying to get him through this.

'What's up?'

Hear air being exhaled. A lot of it.

'Maybe I should have stayed in Feltham.'

'What about the wedding, the reading? You were so keen on it.'

'I ran out of keen.'

'But think of your mam.' Tommy lets loose a cackly sort of laugh. 'Has something happened?'

Silence.

'Is it that girl?'

Silence.

'Are Dad and your mam okay?'

Silence.

'Did you get the wrong deodorant for Christmas?'

'Not even remotely funny.'

I'd asked all the usual questions.

Omerta.

Tommy was saying nothing.

'Well, happy Christmas, Tommy. See you in a week's time.'

He hangs up without so much as a ho-ho-ho.

Christmas has taken a turn for the worse. Sense something bad is about to happen. Don't often get feelings like that, but they're there now, sitting in the pit of me stomach, like undigested pudding.

Mam's sister, Alison, turns up with her husband, Dave, and their four kids, all aged under twelve. The volume in the house suddenly goes through the roof.

Lunch is a happy affair. For everyone apart from me.

Tommy's conversation, or lack of it, has cast a cloud over me. Try to hide how I feel but can tell from Mam and Gran's faces they've spotted it.

'Y'alreet, pet?' says Gran, tapping me hand with a broken Christmas cracker.

'Aye, just thinking about me mocks.'

After dinner go to me room. I need a break from the noise and the jollity. A few moments later, Mam appears. She's not a big drinker, but Christmas is one of those days when her mouth is open for business.

'What is it, sweetheart? Was the turkey a bit dry?'

'Turkey was fine.'

'I'll make sure when it's just us two, everything's cooked perfect.'

It's perfectly, Mam.

'We're going to play charades soon.'

'Great.'

'Bet you've got some amazing book titles stored in that head of yours.'

'Aye.'

'Oh, I do love having you here,' says Mam, leaning in to kiss my cheek, which she somehow misses, planting her lips on me ear. 'Gran and Grandad are so happy you're staying too. Do you like being here?'

Can hardly say no.

'Aye. It's cool.'

Mam starts hiccupping.

'Wait till we get to America, eh?'

Hic.

'What an adventure we'll have.'

Hic.

She puts her drink down on a bedside table that isn't there. The glass falls to the carpet. It's still in one piece. Unlike Mam. She leans across, our bodies joining in the dip our combined weight has caused. She holds me in a tight embrace, the sweet smell of G&T on her breath. A lot more G than T.

Hic.

'I'd like yous to spend more time with me, Ry.'

Hic.

'I've got me mocks soon.'

Hic.

'Oh, and this is a Wi-Fi-free zone is it? Electricity not arrived in Coventry yet?'

Hic.

If this is what alcohol does to you, might stop asking Tommy to take me to the pub.

'Love you so much, Ry.'

Hic.

'Love you too, Mam.'

Hic.

'Know you think I'm being silly. But I'm allowed,' says Mam, fiddling with the ring that's no longer there.

Hic.

Mam grabs me hands. There's a desperate look about her. 'Don't let me down, Ry. Please don't let me down. You're all I've got.'

Hic.

'Another thing.'

After a loud hiccup she whispers in me ear.

'Let you in on a little secret. I'm going to make sure Mark and that woman have a day they'll never forget.'

Hic.

'What do you mean?'

'I'm going to their wedding.'

Teh secrte

'What's up, Tommy?'

Everything.

'Too much homework?' Rock my head back and forward. 'How are the mocks going?'

Badly. I'm right in the middle of them. But haven't done anywhere near enough work. Can't concentrate. The letters in the loft have taken every inch of space in my brain. No room for anything else.

'They're okay.'

'You've just got to...'

Please don't say 'try your best', Mum, please don't say it.

'... apply yourself. Worrying never solved anything.'

Never realised Mum was such a cliché factory. But there's so much I don't know about her.

'Got something for you,' she says.

A confession? But no. It turns out to be her laptop. She opens it on the kitchen table, pulls up a chair and sits next to me. 'I've chosen a new reading for the wedding.'

About time. It's only two weeks until W-Day. She could have given it to me sooner. Only takes five minutes to Google 'wedding readings'. But my anger can wait. My fury is like a bomb I'm constructing day by day, waiting for the moment to detonate and shatter her life, the way she's shattered mine.

Mum finds the link to the reading and turns the laptop my way. I look at a bottle of washing-up liquid instead.

'Not going to read it?'

Don't care about the reading. Or my GCSEs. Or the wedding. Or anything. Or anyone. But I am still her son. The one who tipped a ton of pain on top of her. I swivel my eyes slowly towards the screen.

'How Do I Love Thee', by Elizabeth Barrett Browning.

I read it, but don't read it. The way people like me do.

'What do you think?' says Mum, smiling.

'Okay.'

'Okay, Tommy?' she huffs. 'It's a darned sight better than okay.'

Never heard of this Elizabeth woman. Maybe her words are brilliant. Maybe she's the world's best wedding-reading writer. Don't give a monkey's.

'Sure you'll do an amazing job of it.'

Sure I won't.

'I'll email it to you.'

Send it by carrier pigeon for all I care.

'What on earth's up with you, Tommy?' she says, touching my arm.

'Nothing.'

'Doesn't look like nothing.'

'Just tired.'

Of your lies.

'Told you not to go on your phone at bedtime. The blue light reduces your melatonin.'

Like I care.

Mum squeezes my hand. My hand doesn't return the favour. She can tell I'm not in the mood for mother/son stuff. She gets up, goes to the kitchen cupboards and starts taking out utensils. I watch as she busies herself. I recognise her shape, her hair, her skin. What I don't recognise is her. She's turned into one of those alien words that suddenly appear on a page. The ones I don't understand. Thought I knew my mum. Turns out I never knew her at all.

Trudge upstairs to my room. The place reminds me of my worst days in Feltham, when all the fear and anguish got together to have a party, and I was the only guest. I think of the letters, lying at the bottom of that box above my head. If I'd found them before, perhaps the pain wouldn't have been so bad. I'd have confronted Mum and that would have been that. But the timing's all wrong, with her wedding so close.

Promised I'd never hurt Mum again.

My silence is saving her.

But killing me.

Perhaps that's the price I've got to pay.

But I can't keep that promise for ever.

I'm not strong enough for that.

Wereh's Tmmoy?

The big day.

Make that medium-sized.

A lot of people are missing, the family and friends who chose Mam over Dad. They've taken sides, like people do when war breaks out. Mam's joined the missing list. I made sure of that. I'd like her to have been here. On one condition. She kept her mind open, and her mouth shut. But not sure that would ever happen. I am so relieved she's not coming.

I've got to erase her from me thoughts today. Be happy for Dad and Naomi. She's been dashing around the house all morning, like a kid at Christmas who got a lot more than toiletries and tennis balls. Can see why adults find weddings so exciting. For a day you're the centre of the universe. You have your favourite food and drink. All your best friends and relatives turn up and buy you things. You go on honeymoon. And you marry the person you want to spend your life with. Maybe that's why some people get married more than once.

It's only nine o'clock but I can already hear people bustling noisily around the house. Dad's not among them. He's gone to stay at his friend Charlie's. It's a weird wedding tradition, spending your last unmarried night in a different bed to the person you're marrying. Maybe it's in case one of you wakes up in the morning looking terrible and the other person calls it off. Also keeps him out of a house full of women, all talking shoes, dresses and make-up.

Need to start making meself presentable. Could take some time. I'm not Tommy. Reckon he could crawl out of bed, drag his fingers through his hair and still be Mr Cool. I need to work hard just to look average.

Had me hair cut two days ago. Shouldn't have. They trimmed way too much off. Me big ears now on show for all the world to see.

Long hair suits Ryan better.

Put me dressing gown on and make me way across the landing, past Tommy's door. Tempted to wake him, but don't. He's been acting beyond odd lately. The door remains un-knocked.

Go to the bathroom, lock the door and check meself in the mirror. God, those ears. I spot something else. Little hairs on me chin and upper lip. Never had a shave before but watched Dad enough times. Decide to give it a go. Open his side of the cabinet, take out some gel, a razor and set to work. Are you meant to go up or down with the blade? There's bound to be a shaving video on YouTube. Can't be bothered to find it. Inch the blade tentatively across me face.

Soon realise squinting is no substitute for glasses.

'Damn.'

Blood.

Grab some toilet paper and squish it hard against me chin. Keep dabbing, but every time the paper comes back red. Should have practised this a week before. Maybe a shower will get rid of it. Spend five minutes under steaming hot water, wrap a towel around me and wipe condensation off the bathroom mirror. The little red dot is still there. It's become part of me. Pray it's gone by the time I get to church. At least it'll take eyes away from me ears.

Put me dressing gown on and make me way quickly down the hall. Stop and put one of me oversized ears to Tommy's door. Still no sound. Maybe he got up earlier.

In me bedroom I see the strange-looking outfit hanging on the wardrobe door. Morning suit. Naomi and Dad said they wanted Tommy and me to look our best, as we weren't just readers, we were ushers. I put it on and stare at me reflection. Look like a reject from Eton College. There's a long flappy bit at the back of the jacket that someone forgot to cut off. A shiny waistcoat. Silk tie. Shoes so black, if you turned the light off you'd never find them again.

Check the shaving cut. It's still there. Try dabbing it with a tissue and spit, but it's stubbornly clinging to me chin, like the black spot in *Treasure Island*. Except it's red. And it's on me face. And it doesn't signify guilt. Hope everyone's too wrapped up in the wedding to notice.

Head downstairs. The volume goes up the further I descend. Open the sitting-room door. It's alive with excited voices, what I imagine to be a cross between a women's changing room, a hairdresser's and a spa. Wherever I look there are women having their hair cut or blow-dried, nails done, toenails painted, eyelashes curled, dresses sorted.

I'm the only male here. Before me cheeks can register the fact, a middle-aged woman clocks me.

'Ah, this must be Ryan,' she says. 'Heard so much about you. I'm Grace, Naomi's big sister.'

'Nice to meet you,' I say.

'My, you look a billion dollars. But what's that on your chin?'

'Nowt.'

'It can't be nowt, I can see it. Now, what can we do, eh?' She grabs a tissue from a box, dabs some water on it, and goes to work on me shaving injury. 'Stubborn little bugger, aren't you?' The cut is refusing to budge. 'Here, I'll put a bit of foundation on.'

'I'm fine.'

'Not having you going to my sister's wedding looking like that.'

Want to stop her, but in the blink of an eye, her bag's open, and the foundation is applied.

'That's better, love,' she says, standing back to admire her handiwork.

Need to get out of here, before she finds something else wrong with me.

'Come here, Ryan.'

A voice I know only too well. Naomi, now the epicentre of everyone's attention. She's in her fluffy dressing gown, being attended to by three different handmaidens. One is blow-drying her hair. One is painting her toenails. Another is putting on her make-up.

'Let's have a good look at you.'

I stand in front of her for me inspection, hand resting on me chin, in case the foundation hasn't worked.

'My, don't you look grand.'

No, I look like a pillock, Naomi. But it's your day. And I'm here to serve.

'Have you seen Tommy?' she asks through the reddest pair of lips I've ever seen.

'Not yet.'

'Well, tell him he needs to get a shuffle on. You two have to get to church early, to hand out the Order of Service.'

'I'll go see what he's up to.'

I leave the women to their preparations and clump upstairs to Tommy's room.

Knock. Knock.

'Tommy,' I shout.

No reply.

Might be listening to one of his audio books.

Knock. Knock.

'Are you ready?'

If he is, he's keeping it to himself. Might be in the shower? But the bathroom door is open. No one there. Haven't been in his room for ages. Need to go in now.

Slowly turn the handle.

The door opens.
His morning suit is hanging on the wardrobe door.
His bed is empty.
His room is empty.
Tommy has gone.

Teh dcesiion

Never imagined I'd climb out that window and jump down from that garage roof again. But then I never imagined I'd be in a situation like this again. Where everything's gone wrong. And I need to run.

The winter frost works its way into me. Should have put more clothes on. Not that it matters. Not that anything matters. What's a bit of cold when the person you loved has lied to you, over and over and over, year after year after year? Why did I look at those letters? Because I was practising my reading. Because of *her*. Because of *her* wedding. Because I wanted to make *her* happy for once.

I sit on the swing, thoughts crashing into each other, like dodgem cars. Hear a vibration deep within my coat. Want to ignore it. Want everyone inside it to go away. But phones have always had a hold over me. Can never ignore a message. Might never have ended up inside if it wasn't for my phone, and the stories it told. Pull it from my pocket and look at the screen.

Ryan.

What the hell does he want? Me, of course. Bet he's been dashing round the house, from room to room, like a fly looking for an open window.

Tommy. Anyone seen Tommy?

Want to ignore him. But none of this is his fault.

'Yeah,' I snarl.

'Tommy, where the heck are you?' he says, all breathless.

'At the park.'

'What you doing there? You're meant to be getting ready for church.'

'I'm not going.'

There's a big pause, as Ryan's super-sized brain goes to work.

'But you have to.'

That the best he can come up with?

'Says who?'

'Says... everyone.'

'You do it, Ryan. Don't need me.'

'Wait there.'

Ryan hangs up.

I'm sitting on the swing she was sitting on, all those months ago. Holding the metal chains she held. It's the closest I can get to her. Wish she was here now. She'd know what to do. Close my eyes. Think of us together, before I forced us apart. The good times we had. My mind paints her face, like it used to on those never-ending nights in Feltham. It eases some of the pain.

Open my eyes. In the distance, there's a small man in a suit, running. Not a sight you often see on a Saturday morning. He's coming towards me. As he gets closer, I see that it's Ryan, all dressed up, his coat-tail flapping behind him like a small, black sail. He finally reaches me, panting hard, doubled over with the effort. After gasping in great gob-fulls of cold air, he produces some words.

'Tommy, you've got to get ready,' he pants.

Shrug.

'It's your mam's wedding day.'

'So I see.'

Should I tell Ryan now? Would make life so much easier. Would also make life so much worse. If I tell him, he won't want to go either. That really would detonate Mum's big day.

'Are you just gonna sit here in the freezing cold?'

'Maybe.'

'What's the matter? You told me you wanted to nail your reading to make your mam happy.'

That was before I climbed the ladder into the loft.

'Come on, Tommy. Don't ruin it. It's a big day for me dad too. And you. And me.'

Hadn't thought of Ryan. He's done nothing to deserve this. Sure he loves his mum, but he didn't do anything to stop his dad getting married. He's tried hard to help me read. He moved into a tiny, box bedroom in a house of strangers. Not been easy for him either.

'You could do both readings.'

'No,' shouts Ryan, stamping the blackest shoe I've ever seen. 'You're ready for this. You're gonna do it.' He pulls some paper from his suit pocket. 'I've printed out your reading. Thirty-six point. You could see it from outer space. I've got you a ruler,' he says, pulling it from an inside pocket, 'and a yellow overlay,' he goes, pulling that from another pocket, like a young magician. Only a matter of time before a white dove appears. 'You can't go wrong with these.'

Ryan's like the teacher who's hard to argue with. Rest my forehead on the cold, metal chains. Thinking. Thinking.

'Spoke to Dad. He says there's a lectern in the church. You can put your papers on it and use the ruler. No one will see it. You can do this, Tommy.'

Close my eyes. Imagine the smile on Mum's face. Proud. The son who turned his life around. Maybe she deserves this happy day. Before the unhappy ones to follow.

'Please, Tommy.'

'Okay, stop banging on about it, Ryan. I'll go.'

A smile as wide as the Joker's lights up his face. He leans over and gives me an awkward hug. I get off the swing.

'What's that on your chin? Been in a knife fight?'

'It's nothing.' Ryan looks nervously at his watch. 'You're gonna have to get a move on. We're so late. Run, Tommy, run.'

Ryan's right again.

I turn and sprint for home.

Wddieng Dya nreves

'Bride or groom?'

'Bride.'

As the pews fill up, notice there are far more on Naomi's side of the church than Dad's. If they were getting married on a boat, it would capsize. Reckon Mam would be delighted about this.

I stamp me feet to stay warm in the draughty church porch. Glance at Tommy. He's like a model for a morning-suit company. How can he look that good having spent a fraction of the time getting ready? All the lasses go to him for their Order of Service.

I give him a smile. A tiny upturn of his mouth is me reward. Wish I knew what was going on in that mixed-up head of his. The reading will be over in a blink. No one will even pay much attention to it. They haven't got dressed up, travelled miles, and sat in a refrigerated old building to hear a young guy talk about the meaning of love.

I've tried so hard to lift his confidence, but it would be easier to raise the Titanic. Whatever is up, he's clinging to it as if his life depends on it. Today, Naomi, and everyone else for that matter, are way too wrapped up in the wedding to notice how grumpy he is. When she asked me where Tommy was, I told her he'd gone for a walk, going over his speech.

Dad walks down from the front of the church. He looks great in his suit.

'How's it gannin', lads?'

'Canny.'

Tommy opts for a shrug.

'Next week I'll teach you how to shave, Ryan.'

Naomi's sister needs a more powerful concealer.

Dad pulls up his jacket sleeve and looks at his watch. Haven't seen him this nervous since he told me he and Mam were splitting up.

'Got your readings?' he asks.

Pat me jacket pocket.

Tommy shrugs again.

'Just want to say how proud I am of you both.'

'Thanks.'

Nothing from usher number two. Even Dad, with his nervousness, can't fail to spot Tommy's the opposite of relaxed.

'Is everything okay?'

'Yeah,' he grunts.

Sure you're not meant to lie in church, but as we're standing in the porch maybe it doesn't count. Dad puts a reassuring hand on Tommy's shoulder.

'It's all going to go gangbusters,' says Dad, and he goes back into church to carry on with his fidgeting.

Check me watch. The wedding's due to start at noon. It's now 11.52. In the churchyard, all I can see are rows and rows of dead people. No living people are coming our way.

'Reckon everyone's inside. Shall we take our seats, Tommy?' The guy who's become fluent in shrugging, delivers another one. 'Remember what I said. It's not fear inside you. It's excitement.'

I have never seen anyone look more unexcited than Tommy.

We leave the few remaining Order of Service booklets on a bench in the porch, and walk down the aisle as the organist plays something way beyond me fingers.

'Got everything you need?' I whisper.

'Yeah,' he mutters. 'Everything.'

As we both have speaking parts Tommy and I have places reserved for us, near the front.

We approach our pews.

'You turn right. I turn left,' I say, trying to break the ice.

The ice stays solid. He remains stony-faced.

Touch him on his elbow.

'Good luck, Tommy.'

Dceision tmie

Should have stayed on the park swing.

I'd still be there now if Ryan hadn't come for me. Don't want to be here. Don't want to do what I'm about to do. I put my hand inside my jacket pocket to check the papers. They're still there. Waiting for my moment.

It's not so bad for Ryan. Hardly any of his dad's friends and relatives are here. But Mum's got a full turnout. Her mum and dad, her sister and her husband and kids, aunts, uncles, cousins, some relative from Canada I've never even seen before, except in photos, have all turned up. Then there's all her friends, with their partners and children. To make matters worse, if that's possible, Mum's not only hired a photographer, she's having the whole thing recorded. Everything is going to be caught on film, to be watched over and over.

She's going to regret that.

Should have spoken to Mum. Told her what I'd found. Then she'd understand why I've been acting so strange these last few weeks. Doubt she'd want me to read then.

But typical Tommy, I kept my mouth shut. What is it with me? Had no problem saying yes to Logan and his gang. And yes to Ryan's stupid requests. How come I can't talk to my mum, the person I've known longer than anyone? Maybe we're both too good at keeping secrets. Before my thoughts can beat me up further, the organ music stops.

Then it starts again.

Here comes the bride.

Heads turn, as if there's been an accident. Through the hats and big hair I see her. Instead of Mum there's this amazing-looking woman in a flowing white dress, on the arm of her dad, Grandad Eric. Camera phones click. Mum has a serene smile on her face, like she's the happiest person on the planet.

The polar opposite of me.

Clench my fists. How can I feel so angry on a day like this? I guess anger is a gatecrasher that turns up whenever it likes. I want to forgive her. I want to cut all hate from my heart, at least for today. Put on a performance, the dutiful, loving son. But not sure I can. The hurt she's caused is way too big.

She walks calmly up the aisle, focused on one person, the man in the suit waiting for her with tears in his eyes.

The priest, a short, middle-aged man with a dusting of beard, addresses the crowd.

'The Grace of our Lord Jesus Christ, the love of God, and the fellowship of the Holy Spirit be with you.'

'And also with you,' says everyone.

Apart from me.

He rambles on, his words drifting over me, like smoke.

'We have come together to witness the marriage of Naomi and Mark, to pray for God's blessing on them, to share their joy and to celebrate their love.'

Then my ears prick up.

'First, I'm required to ask anyone present who knows a reason why these persons may not lawfully marry, to declare it now.'

I do.

But it's like in lessons, when the embarrassment of getting it wrong overpowers the chance of getting it right. I keep my mouth shut.

The time isn't right. But it's fast approaching.

And then everyone will know.

Ryn raeds

'I will now call upon Ryan to give the first reading.'

Ease me way past Aunty Freya and Charlie, Dad's best man. Step over a kneeling pad and into the aisle, me heart tapping away at the poem in me pocket. I'm worried. But not for me. For Tommy. I glance back at him, but his head is down, as if he's about to dive off a cliff.

Make me way to the lectern and take out me piece of paper. The reading is neatly laid out.

I've been asked to give readings at school tons of times. Know I'm pretty good at it. Also know something else. This isn't just about me. I decide the reading won't be me best. Not because I don't want Naomi and Dad to be proud of me, but because I don't want Tommy to be shown up. I know how much that would kill him.

Look down at the page. Mam once suggested I joined the school debating society. I learned all about standing tall, speaking loudly, clearly, at a steady pace, giving key words a little extra volume, and how to pause briefly in places, to let the message sink in. Today, I think I'll do things differently.

I begin to speak.

'Let me not to the marriage of true minds admit impediments. Love is not love which alters when it alteration finds.'

I look up briefly from the words. Although me reading merits at best a seven out of ten, I see Naomi and Dad smiling up at me, as if I'm a great Shakespearean actor at the lectern, not a sixteen-year-old boy with big ears and a cut on his chin.

'If this be error and upon me proved, I never writ, nor no man ever loved.'

The end of Sonnet 116.

People don't clap in church, but a sea of smiles tell me it's gone well. Gather the single piece of paper and head back to me seat. Catch Dad's eye. He gives me a thumbs up.

I look at Tommy again. Want to give him some sign of encouragement, but his eyes are still on his shoes. I ease me way along the pew, getting a couple of 'well dones' on the way.

'For the second reading I'd like to welcome Thomas.'

Tmmoy's bg monemt

For a second I wonder who the priest is talking about.

Then realise it's me.

Grandma Ellie nudges me gently with her elbow. The moment I've been thinking about non-stop all these weeks is finally here. I move into the aisle, past Georgia, Mum's best friend, and Hayley, who messed things up for me. Make my way slowly to the lectern. Heart pounding away, I stand behind it, and look at the faces all turned my way. They're not the expressions you get from some of those in class, wishing you to fail, hoping you'll give them a good laugh. They're smiling, encouraging, hopeful.

Take the papers out of my pocket and lean them against the wood.

I grip the lectern and look down at the words.

My dearest Naomi, I'm so sorry I can't be there with you. I hope you can find it in your heart to forgive me.

I have the letters from the loft.

Only decided to bring them this morning, after Ryan found me in the park. What better time, what better place than her own wedding to reveal what Mum did? The words that have been tormenting me are here under the palms of my sweaty hands. I have the explosive device I want. Now all I need is the courage to pull the pin.

Can feel the anger swell within me. But sense something else too. The confusion of the congregation.

Why doesn't he speak?

Because I'm confused too. Why did she do it? Why did she not tell me?

A voice from out there. 'You okay, Tommy?'

Mum.

Daren't look at her. Know if I do, I'll never go through with it. Grip the lectern tighter. Then I spot some words I hadn't seen before. They're written on the top of my reading.

Good luck, Tommy. You'll smash it.

Ryan has broken the spell. I can't go through with it. I can't read the letters. Not now. I promised Mum I'd never hurt her again. This has to wait.

Be of good behaviour.

I take my poem and place it on top of the letters. The words are enormous. I'm sure sixteen point would have done. Don't need the overlay. But slip the plastic ruler from my pocket and place it against the top line. Can sense the eyes on me, the cameras, the phones. Can't destroy Mum's moment. Can't let myself down. Can't let Ryan down.

Feel a bead of sweat. I'm back in my minefield. But I know by treading as lightly as a spider I can reach the other side.

Excitement. Not fear.

A big breath.

Then I begin.

'How do I love thee? Let me count the ways.'

I'm jolted by the shock of hearing myself speak. As if it's someone else. But the moment passes, as moments do, and I relax into the flow. The words are as familiar as the plates I eat off. As I ease through, my excitement increases.

'I love thee freely as men strive for right.'

My voice grows louder. Stronger.

The words are no longer enemies.

I turn a page. The end is in sight. Almost wish Elizabeth had written some more.

'I shall but love thee better after death.'

The end.

Peer over the paper, Mum is beaming at me. She wipes her eyes.

I made the right choice.

For once.

I've made her happy.

If only for a minute.

Hsbaund adn weif

Tommy did a brilliant job.

But don't know why it took him an eternity to get going. He just kept staring at the poem, as if he didn't know what it was. But he did it, handled the pressure of reading out loud in front of so many people on such an important day.

Dead proud of him.

Give him two thumbs up, but he's not looking my way, his eyes once more drawn downwards, shoulders slumped, like a sinner, deep in prayer.

The main event is about to start, the reason all those nails were painted, hats chosen, eyelashes curled, shoes polished, ties knotted and re-knotted, zippers zipped, hair cut and blow-dried, chins shaved, and then covered with foundation.

The wedding vows.

'Mark, will you take Naomi to be your wife? Will you love her, comfort her, honour and protect her, and, forsaking all others, be faithful to her as long as you both shall live?'

'I will.'

A little shiver shoots through me. These are the same promises Dad made to Mam when he married her.

I will became *I won't*.

Reckon they should put marriage vows up around the country. Like speed warnings. Remind people what they should be doing.

Mam pops into me head. So relieved she's not here today. She'd have ruined it. For everyone. But the relief is quickly replaced by worry. What happens when she finds out I've tricked her? Maybe she'll ask for all those Christmas presents back.

Dad and Naomi are gazing into each other's eyes. I want them to stay together. Not just for them, but for me. Don't want to go through this again, Dad finding a new partner, new house, new set of friends. If you do split up, can you hang on a few more years please, until I've left home?

The priest asks Naomi the same question. She gives the same answer.

'I will.'

Watch as they hold out their hands and exchange rings.

'They have declared their marriage by the joining of hands and by the giving and receiving of rings. I therefore proclaim that they are husband and wife.'

Then the bit everyone's waiting for, like the crescendo at the end of a piece of music. Dad and Naomi move close and do a sort of mushy kiss on the lips. You never see a full-on snog at weddings. Think they're banned. Everyone cheers. I join in.

Dad and Naomi go off to sign the register.

The priest says a few more words. Then it's over.

Mr Mark Edward Langley Dyer and Mrs Naomi Emma Cavendish-Dyer walk back down the aisle to some song called 'Happy Talk'. People lean over to grab shots. I can't be bothered. Just let the moment soak in. When Dad and Naomi have passed, everyone starts filing out after them. I follow the crowd outside the church. Everyone is milling about, chatting, laughing.

Everyone that is, except Tommy.

I find him gazing at a gravestone.

'You were dead brilliant,' I say, patting him on the shoulder.

'You were more brilliant,' he mutters.

Even though I wasn't.

'No stumbles or anything,' I say. 'You were a bit slow to get started. What happened?'

'Couldn't find my ruler.'

How hard can it be to find a ruler in a suit pocket? Don't say anything, Ryan. Tommy looks as though he's just stepped out of an exam where all the wrong questions came up. I try to lift his mood.

'Guess we're step-brothers now.'

'Guess so,' he says, without any hint of excitement. His face is impossible to read. Anger/sadness/disappointment/confusion/contempt (delete as appropriate).

Spot the bride and groom making their way towards us. It's slow progress. Everyone wants to offer a kiss, a handshake or a hug.

They finally reach us.

'You two were soooo amazing,' says Naomi, giving Tommy a big squeeze, and a kiss on his cheek for good measure. She breaks free from him and I get a red lipstick mark to go with me red shaving cut.

Dad pumps our hands vigorously up and down as though we've won the Nobel Prize.

'Can I borrow you two for a moment, while the light's still good?'

It's the photographer, looking anxiously upwards as dark clouds edge our way.

'See you guys later,' says Naomi.

The married couple hurry away.

'We'll be heading to the reception soon,' I say, looking at me watch.

'Yeah,' mutters Tommy. 'Where I intend to get smashed.'

Teh reecptoin

'I'd like to give a special mention to our fabulous ushers, Ryan and Tommy.'

Heads turn in our direction. I curl the corners of my mouth into an over-exaggerated smile. 'Didn't they do a good job with the readings?'

Applause ripples across the room. Someone two-finger whistles.

No one, apart from Ryan, has mentioned the long delay before I started reading. The moment will be forgotten. By everyone. Apart from me. When I came so close to destroying the big day.

'Never heard such sweet words come from the mouths of teenage boys.'

Laughter.

Just shut up, Mark.

'Makes a change from...' puts on a terrible impersonation of a teen, "What's for dinner? No, I will not switch my phone off. Why can't my clothes live on the floor? You wouldn't understand."'

Laughter.

'And didn't they look smart. Two male models in the same family.'

More laughter.

'Make that three.'

A bald guy near me bangs his table at the last remark.

You'd better stop now, Mark. You and your stupid little jokes. I have the power to wipe that smug smile off your face.

'Seriously, though, great job, lads,' he says, looking over at us. 'I'm very, very proud of both of you, and so looking forward to the future we have together. Please raise a glass to Ryan and Tommy.'

'To Ryan and Tommy,' booms out.

Glasses clink and Mark continues thanking various people for various things. Though none of them has done anything as significant as me. Managing to keep a secret that's desperate to get out.

'Nice of Dad to thank us,' says Ryan, his face red from all the attention.

Ryan had been nervous about what Charlie, his dad's best man, was going to say. But no mention of his previous marriage, or his mum. As if it never happened.

Flick the cap off another bottle.

The speeches go on and on, like toothache. Can't wait for this to stop, go home, sleep, and try to forget everything. But it's one of those days that's in no hurry to end. Afternoon inches into evening. Wedding meal turns into wedding reception. The B team arrives. All those not invited to the actual wedding turn up in their best clothes, laden with gifts, wearing their finest grins.

Mark and Naomi kick things off with a shuffle around a tiny dance floor. Everyone watches. Apart from me. I stay at the table scraping a label off my bottle of lager. When they've finished, the DJ plays some old music I've never heard before. Whatever it is, the adults like it, and cram into the small space, as if it's a train they're desperate to get on. I won't be joining them. Getting all the exercise I need from my right leg, which is vibrating like crazy.

Open another bottle. Must be a dozen empties in front of me, unless I'm seeing double, and it's only six. Take a swig of warm lager and turn my chair towards the dancefloor. Arms and legs wave around as if trying to fend off a swarm of invisible bees.

Look up. It's someone from Mum's side of the family. Lottie, I think she's called. Her cheeks are flushed. Lottie is teetering on heels she hasn't yet mastered. She's fit. Not that it has any effect on me today.

'Come and dance,' she shouts in my ear.

'Been on the dancefloor loads,' I lie.

Lottie sits down on a chair next to me, her foot touching mine. 'Thought you gave a great speech today.'

'Thanks.'

'Love your voice.'

'Cheers.'

'Who was the poem by?'

'Elizabeth somebody.'

'Cool. I love poetry.'

'Great.'

'Sure you don't want to dance?'

'Positive.'

Lottie looks crestfallen.

'See you later, Tommy.'

She brushes my shoulder with her fingers and wobbles off to find someone else. Feel bad. Must have taken some guts to come over to a guy she's never met and ask for a dance. She only wants a bit of fun. The one thing I don't want right now.

I pick up my bottle and take a slug. Reckon I'd fail Ryan's eyesight test. The room has gone into soft focus. People look like smudged drawings. But the drink has failed to lift my spirits. What makes it worse is watching everyone having the time of their lives, laughing, joking, jostling, singing. Don't think Mum's even noticed the old Tommy isn't at the wedding.

I watch her. She's changed out of her wedding dress, into a sparkly thing that is the opposite of flowing. She's dancing in the middle of a group of girlfriends, a jumble of arms and legs and hair.

Sense someone sit next to me. It's Ryan.

'Haven't seen you on the dancefloor,' he pants.

'That's because I haven't been on the dancefloor.'

He looks like a city worker who's decided to run to the office, his suit buttons undone, tie all wonky, his face red and sweaty.

'You can take stuff off, you know.'

Ryan undoes the knot on his tie, removes it from his neck, and shoves it in his pocket.

'So hot out there,' he says, grabbing a bottle from the table, and removing the cap.

The alcohol froths out. Ryan puts his mouth over the

top, but only succeeds in giving himself a lager wash. The bubbles finally turn to liquid. Ryan raises his bottle.

'Cheers.'

We clink.

'Cheers,' I mumble.

I sit watching a young girl, feet planted on her dad's shoes, as they slide around the edge of the dancefloor. Not a care in the world.

'You can relax now, Tommy. You did it.'

If only it was that easy. A short reading. Pats on the back. Life back to normal.

I look at him as he stares out, smiling at all the people, shaking what they've got.

Ignorance is bliss.

Never really understood that saying, until now. Ryan is totally unaware of the knowledge eating away at me. He simply has no idea. Sharing it will kill his happiness stone dead. I don't want to do it, but I can't carry it around any longer. It's too big a burden. He has to know. Has a right to know.

Thought long and hard about the best time to tell him. Problem is, there's no best time. There are only wrong times. I'd decided, when I was up there at the lectern, I was going to leave it until after the wedding. But that's now.

'What's the matter, Tommy? You look so... angry?'

Because I am.

Can't do it here, with all the noise, and music and laughter. Not with them around.

'Ryan, want you to come outside with me.'

'Why? It's freezing.'

I lean in close to him. 'I'm asking you to come outside.'

Can see fear in his eyes. 'Have I done something wrong?'

Shake my head.

The tension leaves him. 'Okay, then.'

We get up from the table and make our way through bodies all moving erratically as a result of Abba and alcohol. Reach the door. I push it open and my face is punched by a blast of cold air. Feel myself sway. Hold yourself together, Tommy. Almost there.

Need to get as far away from the merriment as possible. I keep walking, across a patio, down some steps, out on to the cricket pitch. Hear Ryan behind me, his feet audible on the crispy, frozen grass.

'Why have we come all the way out here?'

You'll find out soon enough.

I stop and face him. Glad I've had all those bottles. Not sure I'd be doing this if I was sober. There's enough moonlight to see his face. He looks pensive, curious, afraid. No idea how he'll take the news.

'Ryan, I have something to tell you.'

His eyes narrow behind his glasses.

'I've discovered something.'

'What?'

'Your dad. My mum. They're my parents.'

Angare nda cnfousin

The stupid Tommy's back.

The one who joins gangs.

The one who goes to prison.

'How much have you had to drink?' I ask.

'Not enough.'

'This isn't funny, Tommy.'

'Too right, it's not.'

I stare at his face, expecting it to change shape any second, and a laugh to burst from his lips. It never comes. He stares at me. There's no humour in his eyes. Only sadness.

'Who told you that?' I say, still refusing to believe a word.

'No one told me. I found them in the loft. Letters from your dad to my mum. I brought some with me. Was going to read them out in church. Humiliate her for what she's done. That was my plan when I got up there. But couldn't bring myself.'

He pulls a sheaf of papers from his pocket and gives them to me.

Take them with shivering hands.

He takes out his phone and uses the light to illuminate the letters.

I recognise the writing.

Dad's.

Naomi, I so wish I could be with you at the birth. My heart breaks to think of you going through this on your own. I wish you'd told me earlier. When our son is born I'll do all I can to help. I'm there for you if you ever need me.

'How do you know this is you he's talking about?'

'Look at the date on the top of the letter.'

Do the maths in me head.

It would make the boy exactly the same age as… Tommy.

Taste wedding cake as it takes the elevator up to me throat.

'Oh, my God.'

'There are more letters, after the birth. Talking about their son, Tommy. If you don't believe me, climb into our loft. They're in a red shoebox in the left-hand corner. All the evidence you need is there.'

Feel light-headed. Even though I've only had a few lagers.

This can't be true.

But it makes a horrible sense. Why Dad decided to come south when he and Mam divorced. Why he was so keen for us to move in with Naomi. Why they both kept trying to make us be friends. Why Dad went off on bond-building bike rides with Tommy. Why Tommy's been acting a total weirdo these last few weeks.

Another thought pushes to the front of the queue. Was Tommy the reason Mam and Dad separated? Can't be. If Mam had known that she'd have said so. Would never keep something like that to herself. But if she didn't know, why had Dad kept the secret locked up for so long?

'Why didn't they tell us?' I yell.

Tommy folds his arms, and shrugs. 'You tell me.'

Clouds of breath leave me.

Feel cold. Really cold.

More thoughts barge their way in. Mam and Dad had me after Tommy was born. Which means Dad decided to have another kid, when he already had one. Why would he do that? For sixteen years he let me believe I was an only child, when me brother lived three hundred miles away.

Me actual, 3-D, living, breathing brother, is standing right in front of me. This is way too much for me brain to cope with.

I look at Tommy. Can tell he's as angry and confused as I am.

'I'm going to speak to them.'

'No, Ryan. Not now. Leave it.'

But I'm not listening to him.

I turn and hurry towards the bright lights of the cricket club.

The offeic

Should never have told him. Correction. Should have told him. Just not today. That's what happens when you drink. Common sense goes on holiday.

I'd decided to confront them tomorrow. Or maybe the day after that. But the cat is out of the bag and running across the grass towards the cricket club.

'Stop,' I shout.

But it's too late. The letters have already gone to work on Ryan, the way they did with me. He's at the door. I catch up and grab him by the shoulder.

'It won't do any good,' I shout, spinning him around.

'Who said it has to be good?'

'Leave it. Till you've calmed down.'

But he's way beyond caring. Can see a madness in his eyes I've never seen before. He squirms out of my grasp, grabs the door handle and goes inside. The party's created a wall of noise. It breaks over me like a wave. I begin to shake, even though it's roasting in there. Should have gone home sooner. Too late for that. Too late for everything.

I follow Ryan into the mess of bodies. His head swivels this way and that, looking for his dad, my dad. I barge my way through the throng, trying to keep up with him. See his head twisting this way and that, his feet on tiptoes, searching for his target. He moves towards the bar. I follow close behind. But not too close. This is Ryan's idea. Not mine. Watch as he grabs his dad by the arm, spilling his beer.

'What are you doing, Ryan? I'm talking to Neil,' he shouts, to make himself heard above the noise.

Ryan would apologise in normal circumstances. But these circumstances are about as abnormal as you can get.

'I need to talk to you and Naomi. Now.'

Not sure if it's Ryan's words, or the volume at which he delivers them, but Mark puts down what's left of his beer.

'Excuse me, Neil.'

Follow Mark and Ryan as they seek out the bride. Mum is sitting with a gaggle of girlfriends. Shrieks of laughter cut through the music.

Mark bends and whispers in her ear. She gets unsteadily to her feet. Mum is precariously balanced on heels as thin as nails. She waves goodbye to her friends, before staggering after Ryan and her new husband.

Mark opens a door at the side of the bar and all four of us go inside a tiny office, bursting with everything you need to run a cricket club – boxes, bats, pads, papers, fixture lists, and stuff scattered about, still looking for a home. It reminds me of the loft.

Mum sits clumsily on a chair, almost missing it completely. She shuffles her bum so she's parked safely.

'This better be important,' she says, blinking as she tries to bring Ryan and me into focus. 'I'm not done with dancing yet.'

'Oh, it's important all right,' says Ryan, glaring at Mum. 'We want to know when you were going to tell us.'

And in that instant they know.

Mum slumps forward and begins to cry.

Turth adn lise

'Tell us, tell us,' I scream.

I never raise me voice. But I'm raising it now.

Dad and Naomi look shocked to the core.

'How did you find out?' mumbles Dad.

The heavy thump of bass reverberates through the walls, and through me stomach.

I pull out the letters Tommy found. No longer smooth, but completely crumpled, only worthy of the bin.

'Your old love letters.'

I hurl them to the floor.

Naomi and Dad swap looks, like two criminals in the dock, as the damning evidence is revealed.

We're going down.

'You shouldn't have kept them,' says Dad, glaring at Naomi.

'What else did I have of yours?' she sobs.

'You had me.'

They both turn to Tommy, as though realising for the first time their son is in the room.

Naomi's crying goes up a level. 'We wanted to tell you. We wanted things to work out,' she says, two little rivulets running down her face. 'But...'

'But what?'

The music breaks through the door.

Naomi's words dry up.

Dad steps up to the crease. 'Things were complicated, Ryan. I was married to your mam when it happened.'

'Why did you stay with her if you loved Naomi so much?'

Dad runs his hand over his face, as if he's been wrestling with the same question for all these years. And never found an answer.

'It's not his fault,' says Naomi, her words filling Dad's silence. 'When I found out I was pregnant, I didn't tell Mark.'

'Naomi...'

'Please, Mark.' She squeezes her hands tight. 'It was my mistake.'

'That's my new name now, is it... Mistake?'

'No, Tommy. It's not like that.'

'So what is it like?' he says, his face flushed with anger.

'Mark had been sent to London for a few months to open a new office. We met. We had an affair. He went back up north. We decided to call a halt to things. And then you came along. Unplanned.'

'That's great, isn't it?' screams Tommy, picking up a cricket bat and swinging it at a big stack of papers. They scatter across the floor.

Never seen this Tommy before. Wide-eyed, furious. The type you'd expect to see in a gang.

'I'm so sorry, Tommy,' says Naomi.

'We'd stopped seeing each other,' says Dad. 'Then I got a call one day from Naomi. Said she's soon to give birth. Then shock number two.' Dad's eyes momentarily flick across to me. 'Katie's pregnant with Ryan.'

'So I wasn't wanted either?'

'Course you were, Ryan. It was just... so, so bloody complicated.'

Dad rubs his eyes, hardly able to believe what he did all those years ago is now alive in this room.

'Your dad thought of leaving Katie,' says Naomi, looking up at me. 'I said no. Ryan had brought them back together again. He had his wife, his son, his job, up north. I told him I'd bring Tommy up on my own.'

Her words stop, replaced by the monotonous thump from next door. It's crazy. In the next room people are dancing, laughing, drinking, celebrating Mark and Naomi's happiness. And here, the polar opposite. The bride and gloom.

I look from Dad to Tommy. Same height, same dark hair, same lean bodies, same blue eyes.

How come I never saw it?

Famyil tise

Haven't seen her cry like this since I was sent to prison. Saving it all up for today.

'I'm so sorry, Tommy,' she wails. 'Maybe I should have done things differently. But I didn't want to wreck Mark's marriage.'

'It's wrecked anyway,' mutters Ryan.

'It wasn't then.'

I glare at Mark. 'You just walked away,' I shout, using the bat to hit a pair of cricket pads across the room.

'Tommy, put the bat down,' says Mum.

Be of good behaviour.

Feels like a bad behaviour sort of day.

I keep hold of it.

'I didn't walk away, Tommy. I paid towards your school fees and helped out financially.'

'What?' exclaims Ryan, 'so while I'm at state school, he goes to private school.'

'That's what guilt does to you, Ryan.'

Neither Mark nor Mum correct me.

'I wanted to do something for Tommy,' mutters Mark.

'Birthday card might have been nice.'

'Tommy, Mark couldn't do anything like that. He was trying to keep his marriage together, for Ryan's sake.'

'Oh, well, as long as Ryan's happy.'

'Please, sweetheart—'

'Please, what, Mum? You lied to me. You said you had a one-night stand with some stranger. Seems like a lot more than one night. And he certainly wasn't a stranger.'

Mum says nothing, scratching at a red wine stain on her dress.

'So how come you suddenly decided to get back together?' I say, cradling the bat in my hands.

They swap looks again, praying one of them knows the answer.

'We never lost touch,' says Mark. 'I stopped sending letters. But over the years we swapped emails. I was desperate to know what was going on. Naomi would send me pictures. I even went to watch you play football.'

'You never told me that,' says Mum, shocked.

'I needed to see him. Told Katie I was taking part in another triathlon. Drove down here instead.'

Weird to think my secret dad was on the sidelines, next to all the non-secret dads.

'But everything changed the day you got arrested.'

'My fault again, is it?'

'It's no one's fault, Tommy,' says Mum. 'I called Mark, told him what happened. He said he's going to get a job down in London. We started meeting. Realised how much we still felt for each other. How much catching up we had to do. I asked Mark to move in.'

'Thought your delinquent son needed a father figure?'

'Not ashamed to say it, Tommy,' says Mark, 'I felt so much guilt at the way things worked out. Or didn't work out.'

Thump. Thump. Thump.

Hard to tell where the music stops and my headache begins.

'When were you going to tell us?' asks Ryan.

Mum looks to Mark again. 'We were going to wait until after your GCSEs. Didn't want anything to disrupt your studies.'

Ryan joins me in the laugh-making department.

'You thought exams were more important than this?'

'No. We just wanted to choose our moment.'

But the moment had other ideas.

'Does Mam know?' asks Ryan, his voice wavering.

Mark looks at his ultra-black shoes and shakes his head. 'No, she doesn't.'

'When were you going to tell her?'

'Once we'd told you.'

Thump. Thump. Thump.

'We didn't want things to turn out like this, Tommy. They just happened.'

I look at Mum. She carried me for nine months. She carried her lie for seventeen years. Can I ever trust her again?

'I want to go home, Mark,' she says, her face as crumpled as their love letters.

'We can't, sweetheart. Not yet. There are one hundred and fifty people out there.'

Mum begins crying again. 'What do we tell everyone?' she says, great sobs breaking from her lips.

'We say we wanted a private chat, somewhere quiet, to thank the guys for their amazing speeches.'

Mark gets A-star for lying. But then he's had plenty of practice.

'Go to the ladies', get yourself sorted,' he says. 'I'll get the DJ to do some slow dances. Just you and me. Then we can say you're feeling ill and need to go.'

Mum forces a smile. But can tell it doesn't want to be there.

'I'm sorry you two had to find out this way,' says Mark. 'I don't blame you for being furious. We can get through this.'

Who's we? I have no intention of ever getting over this.

Mark lifts Mum from her seat and wraps an arm around her. Bet he never thought his wedding reception would end like this. Mum wipes her eyes. He turns the handle and releases all the fun and the laughter dammed behind the door. They disappear into the noise.

The door closes behind them. The fun and laughter gone.

Look at Ryan.

He looks destroyed.

I put the cricket bat down and give him a hug.

'You and I will get through this.'

'What makes you think that?'

'We're brothers.'

Mma's aengr

'Ryan, it's Mam.'

Damn.

'I'm outside the church. There's neebody here.'

She moves her phone around to show me the deserted graveyard of St Bartholomew's Church.

'Aye, you're right. There's neebody there.'

The camera returns to her heavily made-up face. On her head sits a big flowery hat.

'Where are they, Ryan?' seethes Mam, with enough venom to poison a whole town.

No easy way out of this.

Deep breath.

'The wedding was last Saturday.'

Her eyes bulge.

'You what?'

'It was last Saturday, Mam. Must have given you the wrong date. By mistake.'

'Mistake, my bum. You did it deliberately,' she screams.

Hold the phone away from me. She doesn't look so scary when she's smaller.

I've been angry with Mam. But the anger's now replaced by sadness. I know what Dad did behind her back. The double life he's been living. A life she knew nothing about.

'Yeah, I did it deliberately, Mam. Didn't want you ruining Dad and Naomi's day.'

I managed that all by myself.

If she'd shown up last week it would have been a major disaster. She'd probably have arrived late, sneaked in the back of the church, keeping quiet. But she wouldn't have stayed silent for long. She'd have said something, or more likely, shouted something. There'd have been a big scene, ending with her being bundled out the building. Dad fuming. Naomi crying.

If that had happened Tommy might have kept his news to himself. His mam and our dad punished for what they'd done. But it's not how the story played out. And here we are, still waiting for the perfect ending.

'Who are you to say how I was going to behave?'

'You weren't invited, Mam. They didn't want you there.'

'And neither did you.' She looks crushed, as if the weight of the last few years has got too much for her. 'Thought you were the one person I could rely on. You've betrayed me.'

Know what I did was wrong. Know what I did was right.

'I'm sorry, Mam, but I didn't betray you. I did what I felt was best.'

'For who?'

'For everyone. Including you.'

Never spoken to Mam like this before. Maybe I've gone too far.

'Do you want me to come and meet you?'

'No, Ryan, I do not,' says Mam. 'You've humiliated me.'

'No, I haven't. You got dressed up and made a journey you didn't have to. But if you want to feel humiliated, go ahead.'

'You're just like him. You're a bastard and a liar.'

She hangs up.

'If only you knew, Mam.'

Mam's never sworn at me before. Ever. Tears prick me eyes. Didn't want things to come to this. I only did it to save her. Perhaps there's a silver lining to this black cloud. She'll never want to go to America with me now. She may never want to see me again.

But that's not what I want either.

I need us to have a proper relationship. Not this pretend one we've been having.

Things need to change.

Teh turth abuot Tmmoy

The wintery sun is sneaking into my room.

Nice day, people will say. Could do with one of those. The last seven have been horrific. Those ten minutes in the cricket office polluted everything. Not sure how Mum and Mark managed to carry on with their reception after that. But they did. Guess they'd got good at acting. Afterwards they went to a hotel somewhere. Bet they were glad they didn't have to share a taxi home with Ryan and me. That would have been the icing on their wedding cake.

I fell asleep in the cab, apparently snoring my head off, and dribbling down my suit. Ryan, who'd got stuck into the free lager, threw up. The cab driver made us pay an extra fifty quid.

They came back the following morning, looking the opposite of how they did at the wedding: pale-faced, dishevelled, distraught. Couldn't even get their miserable faces to look at us when they walked through the front door. There followed an endless procession of 'sorries'. As if that's somehow going to fix everything. They then went off to the Lake District for a short honeymoon. Glad to have them out of the house.

Get dressed and go downstairs. Ryan's on the sofa wearing his T-shirt with funny Scandinavian words on it, creased boxers and a pair of battered tartan slippers. His face is white, eyes red, his body hunched like he's about to give someone a piggy-back. On the plus side, the cut on his chin has gone.

'Okay?' I say, realising how stupid this sounds the second it leaves my mouth.

'Opposite of okay,' he mumbles. Ryan pulls his knees up to his chest. 'Me mam turned up at the church.'

'You what?'

'I told her the wedding was today.'

'Oh, man, that's ace,' I say, slapping my thigh. Get up to fist-bump Ryan, but his hands stay wrapped around his knees. I fist-bump his foot.

'Nothing to be proud of, Tommy.'

Ryan's right. I know only too well how lying to your mum can hurt.

'But you couldn't have her screw up the wedding. You did the right thing.'

'Doesn't feel like the right thing.'

I sit on the floor in front of him. 'Don't worry about your mum, she'll get over it.'

'What, like we've totally failed to get over this?'

Ryan's right again.

'Don't beat yourself up, man. You helped me with my reading, stopped your mum messing up the wedding, and had the balls to confront Mum and Mark. You did good.'

Can't believe I'm trying to boost Ryan's confidence. But before I start going through all the things he's better at than me, hear the front door open.

'Hello,' shouts Mum.

Ryan and I keep our mouths shut.

The door opens to reveal the married couple. Their cheeks are red from too much weather. Don't bother asking how it was. Five days of fresh air and recriminations.

They find chairs and flop down. We sit, like people on the underground, trying to avoid each other's eyes. Mum finally takes a deep breath and speaks. 'Just wanted to say sorry guys... again. We want to apologise for what we did. Or rather didn't do,' she says, twisting the sparkly ring on her finger. 'The longer it went on the harder it became to admit it.'

'Yeah, so you said.'

'Please, Tommy,' says Mark.

He looks at his new wife, then back to his sons.

'We came so close, so many times, but we thought, it's best if you two got to know each other first.'

Mum singles me out for eye contact. 'Your dad and I love you both so much.'

'If you love him so much why did you make him read in front of all those people, when you know he can't?'

'Ryan,' I shout.

'They need to know.'

'What does he mean?' says Mum, confused.

'Tommy's dyslexic,' he mumbles.

'What?' exclaims Mum.

'Yeah, he struggles with reading, especially out loud.'

'But he read brilliantly,' exclaims Mark.

Told Ryan to never talk about this. But what's the point? Been way too many lies lately.

'Yeah, thanks to Ryan,' I say. 'He helped me with the reading. Both readings.'

The news electrocutes Mum. She sits bolt upright. 'How come I didn't know that?'

I could tell her it's because I'd become an expert at keeping secrets, like she did. That I caused trouble. That I hid behind other talents. That I'd ask a question at the start of a lesson, so I wouldn't be asked later. That I pretended to hate English. But I'm not going to. Not after what she did.

'Maybe you had other things on your mind,' I say.

An invisible lightbulb goes on over her head.

'That's why you got thrown out of those schools, isn't it? It wasn't bad behaviour. It was because you struggled to read or write.'

Ten out of ten, Mum.

'We can get you help for it,' says Mark.

Your sort of help I can do without.

I get up from the floor, storm out of the room, and slam the door shut.

Ryn's adveic

Heard nothing from Mam.

Sent texts.

Tried calling.

It's one-way traffic.

Not told Dad that I stopped Mam coming to his wedding. I'll tell him sometime, when things have calmed down. Which probably won't be for several years. Might even make things worse. If that's possible. Sometimes silence is the only answer.

I need to speak to someone about what's going on. Someone other than Tommy.

After a dozen laps of me room, I gather enough courage to pick up me phone.

Find the number I'm looking for.

Ring. Ring.

'Hello.'

'Hi, Gran, it's Ryan here.'

'Eeh, hello, pet. How lovely to hear from yous.'

'Is Mam there?'

'She's in the front room. I'll gan fetch her.'

'No, no, please, no. It's you I want to talk to.'

'Me?'

'Aye, you.'

Gran's chest is a bit wheezy. Her sharp intake of breath is loud and clear. Reckon she knows what this is about.

'Okay, spit it out,' she says.

'I'm worried about me mam.'

'Not the only one, love.'

'You know she came down… to Dad's wedding.'

'The little bugger. Told me she was gannin' to a christening.'

'There was no harm done. I told her the wrong day.'

A half-laugh, half-cough.

'Your Grandad and I wondered why she came back in such a foul mood, spitting feathers she was, like she'd swallowed a turkey. Spent the whole afternoon sulking in the conservatory, listening to Mozart. We thought it was odd. Mean, you can't get angry at a christening, can you?'

'I've tried getting in touch. She won't return me calls, texts, nothing.'

Another great chesty sigh. 'Your mam's gannin' through a bad patch, Ryan, what with everything that's gannin' on. I think the wedding's the straw that broke her back. And she misses you like mad. Never seen her as happy as when you were up at Christmas.'

'And now she won't even speak to me.'

A pause as Gran gathers her thoughts.

'Suggest you just keep deein what you're deein, pet. Send her messages. Tell her you love her.'

'And that'll do the trick?'

'Nothing's certain in this world. But I know your mam better than anyone. While she can be as stubborn as a stick, she sees reason eventually.'

Never had a conversation like this with Gran before.

'When will that be?'

'How long's a piece of string? The most important thing is you let her know you're thinking about her. Being there for someone is the best thing you can do. Sometimes it's the only thing you can do.'

'Thanks so much, Gran.'

'You're welcome, pet.'

'Tell her I called, asking after her.'

'I will.'

About to say me goodbyes when Gran coughs up a final question.

'One more thing, while I've got you, Ryan.'

'What's that?'

'How was the wedding?'

Teh offre

Lie on my bed, reading. Not for study, for relaxation. Never thought I'd do that in a billion years, but then I never thought I'd live in a house with my actual dad, and my actual brother. It's been two weeks since the wedding. They say time heals. Not sure eternity can cure this. Still angry at Mum, Mark, the world. Can't bring myself to call him Dad. Those three little letters form in my head, but they can't make the short journey to my mouth.

The atmosphere in our house is like Feltham. Even when things are calm, you know we're only a word away from them kicking off. We've become warring armies, manoeuvring around each other as best we can. Occasionally we meet, and there are hostilities. But, despite the size of the house, we've become good at avoiding each other. It's better that way.

Knock. Knock.

Too gentle to be Ryan.

'Can I come in?'

Mum.

Don't want to let her in. But it's her house.

'Okay.'

Put my book face down on the bed. Mum appears. She's wearing her workout gear. She grabs the chair from under my desk and pulls it over to the side of my bed.

'Reading?'

Nod.

'What is it?'

'A book.'

An actual book.

'Know I've said it before, but I'm going to say it again, and keep on saying it until we're all sick and tired of hearing it. I'm sorry, Tommy, I am so gobsmackingly, heart-achingly, soul-searchingly—'

'Okay, get the point.'

Silence.

'Your dad and I...'

'Can you stick to Mark, please.'

'Mark and I have been talking. You and Ryan have done a great job keeping things quiet. But they can't stay under wraps for ever. It's time for the lying to stop. We're going to break the news.'

Mum looks up at my ceiling, blinking back tears.

'Not going to be easy, but we're going to organise a lunch with close family. Don't worry, you don't have to come. We'll tell them then.' Mum tugs at her leggings. 'On the same day, I'll notify the school. Best everyone hears at once.'

'What you gonna say?'

'The truth. We thought it best for all concerned if we kept it secret. Until now.'

'Can you stop saying "best for all concerned". It was best for you and him. No one else benefitted from this. No one.'

Can tell my words have hurt her. Don't care.

Mum sits staring at my revision timetable. As though it's actually interesting.

'What about Ryan's mum? When's she going to find out?'

'Mark's going to see her on the day of the lunch. After the lunch.'

Only met Ryan's mum once, but in a funny sort of way we're united. Tied together by this gigantic lie.

'Hope she gives him hell.'

'Don't blame Mark for all this, Tommy. I'm as culpable as him. We're in it together. We all do things we regret.'

Don't we just.

She forgave me for what I did. Can I ever forgive her?

'I also came to apologise about something else. For not spotting your dyslexia. How could I not have known? You were doing so well, what with your football scholarship and your drama, and your art. I remember teachers saying your reading and spelling wasn't great, but never made the connection. Then I ask you to do a reading to a church full of people. How stupid can you get? I'm so sorry, Tommy.'

Hated Mum for putting me through that. But how was she to know? I always made myself out to be Mr Super Confident. Mum must have thought reading a few words out loud would be a piece of cake for someone like me.

'Wish the school had flagged it up more.' She shakes her head. 'Thank heavens for Ryan is all I can say.'

Who'd have thought the guy who'd been such a pain would end up saving the day. Rescued by my very own brother.

'I've been talking to your da— Mark about it. We'd like to get you properly assessed, see what can be done before your GCSEs.' She looks at the book on my bed. 'Though judging by that, you're doing pretty well already.'

Don't be so sure, Mum. It's in extra big type.

'What do you say, Tommy? Can we help?'

Part of me wants to fling the offer straight back in her face. But a different part wants to take it. Don't want to go through life stumbling over words, swerving books, making mistakes, scared to read out loud.

'Yeah, I'm up for it.'

Rcenciliotian

The day of the big reveal.

Can normally tell what sort of mood me dad's in by the noise of the front door closing.

This is a doozy.

Wham.

If we had glass in the door, we'd now be calling the glazier. Three weeks after their best day ever, they're having their worst day ever. Having to explain the inexplicable. That was one lunch I'm glad I wasn't invited to.

Hear them shuffling around in the hall. Not talking.

Silence is far worse than shouting.

Dad walks into the sitting room where Tommy and I are playing a video game. We put our controls down the second Dad comes in. Can tell from his face that it didn't go well.

'And now the highlight of me day,' he sighs, 'meeting your mam.'

'Can I come?'

Dad looks shocked.

'No, Ryan, you cannot. It's going to be tricky. Trust me.'

'I don't care.'

And I really don't. Been so much fighting between Mam and Dad, another battle won't make much difference. Even one as big as this.

'I don't want you there when I break the news.'

'I'll go into another room.'

Dad laughs. 'Another room? If you were in another county you'd still hear it.'

'I said I don't care.'

Dad looks defeated, deflated, despondent, and probably a few other d words as well. He's all out of arguing.

'Okay, grab your coat.'

He leaves the room.

'Are you insane?' mutters Tommy. 'Why would you go all that way to watch them scream at each other?'

'I want to see me mam.'

She still hasn't spoken to me since turning up at the empty church for the wedding that wasn't. I keep going over the advice Gran gave me. About being there for people. Don't want to be the type who turns their back when things go wrong. Been sending her messages. Yet to get one back. But it's not just Mam who needs support. Dad does too. I'm not as good at staying angry as Tommy. Feel sorry for Dad. See how miserable this has made him. Must be the worst start to married life ever. Things may never be a 100 per cent normal again, but I reckon they can get to 50 per cent. Which is still a pass.

Wonder what would have happened if I hadn't taught Tommy how to read. He wouldn't have been tempted to go through those letters in the loft, and the storm would have passed. Okay, we'd have found out on GCSE results day in August. It would still have been a punch to the face, but at least it wouldn't be in the middle of a wedding. We'd be older. And wiser. Maybe.

I run to the car before I change me mind.

The first few miles vanish in total silence. We're like those old couples you see in cafés, staring into space, having run out of things to say. Dad has his ring on. Thought he might take it off today. Suppose he realises there's no point. You can hide an affair, but you can't hide a wedding.

Dad's been in third gear twelve times before he speaks.

'I'm glad you came, Ryan. It's been hell these last few weeks.'

'How did the lunch go?'

Dad snorts a laugh, and wipes spit off the steering wheel. 'Every bit as bad as you'd expect. We had everything. Shock. Disappointment. Scowls. Arguments. The manager came with the bill before pudding. Said we were upsetting the other guests.' Shakes his head at the memory. 'Never been so glad to get a bill in me life. And now I'm about to get me desserts.'

At least his sense of humour is intact.

Look out at flooded fields. Grey skies. Wonder what the weather's like in New York now. Not that Mam will ever be taking me there.

'Does she know? I mean, anything?'

Dad stares straight ahead as if he hasn't heard.

'She knew I had an affair.'

'But still took you back?'

'Yeah. Said she still loved me. Wanted to make a go of it. You were the end result. Then find out Naomi's eight months pregnant and Mam's pregnant with you. Talk about good timing, eh?'

'Did Mam know Naomi gave birth to Tommy?'

Dad shakes his head.

Another question that's been gnawing away at me.

'If you'd found out sooner that Naomi was pregnant, would you still have had me?'

'What a question, Ryan.' He reaches across and touches my hand. 'I'm so glad we did.'

Neatly swerved giving an answer.

Weird to think I wouldn't be here now if Dad and Mam had separated. I'd be officially nothing. The only part of me that might still be alive is me name. They obviously both liked it enough to give it to me, so if either of them had had a boy with someone else he'd probably be called Ryan. But he'd be a different Ryan to the one sitting here. Biology is strange like that.

'What you thinking about?' he asks.

Too weird to explain.

'Nowt.'

Silence.

'Your mam loves you very, very much.'

And she hates you very, very much.

That's something no one's arguing about.

We don't talk about the situation anymore. Dad asks about school, and mock GCSEs, and Tommy. Imagine his brain wants to do anything other than think about the conversation to come.

We reach Gran and Grandad's house. They come to the front door, but don't bother coming down the path.

'Hi, Ryan.'

With enthusiasm.

'Hello, Mark.'

With none.

They don't seem their normal bubbly selves. Maybe they've had a premonition of what's to come. We walk into the house, as if we're going to a funeral. Dad's.

We stand there in the hall, like strangers in a lift.

'She's in there,' says Grandad, motioning towards the front room.

Dad nods, then pauses, steeling himself. He turns the handle and goes in. Gran and Grandad usher me into the dining room. The instrument of torture sits waiting for me. Still haven't told Mam I've given up me lessons. So glad I did. No longer having to spend hours putting me fingers in positions they don't want to go. Not feeling Mrs Grayling's stale breath on me neck. But there's no escape at Gran and Grandad's. I'll do me best. For them.

'Can we have a bit of Rodgers and Hammerstein, pet?' asks Gran.

'What did they write?'

Gran laughs. 'What didn't they write, more like. *Carousel*, *South Pacific*, *The King and I*. And, our favourite, *The Sound of Music*.'

God, no. Remember watching that one Christmas. Said I hoped the Germans captured the Von Trapp family. Thought Gran was going to kill me. But haven't come up here to start a war. *The Sound of Music* it is. I grab the piano book and turn to 'My Favourite Things'. I'm rusty, but Gran and Grandad don't seem to care, coming up with words I'm sure neither Rodgers nor Hammerstein wrote.

The only benefit of playing is it drowns out most of the sounds from next door. But every now and then, Mam's voice breaks through the walls, unleashing all that pent-up anger that's been bottled up. Someone should write a musical about Mam and Dad. *The Sound of Arguing*.

I'm halfway through another piece when the dining-room door opens. Dad stands there, looking like he did after the pub lunch.

'Would yous like a cuppa, Mark?'

Gran always offers a cup of tea when things are bad. It's gonna take more than a tea bag to fix this.

'No, thanks, Hilary. Going for a little walk. Clear me head.' Dad turns to me. 'Your mam wants a word with you.'

Can't imagine it's just one.

Close the music book and follow Dad into the hall. I look at the dining-room door, scared of what I'll find on the other side.

'How is she?' I whisper.

'You'll be fine.'

Not what I asked.

'Enjoy your walk,' I say.

He looks close to tears. I've not seen him cry before.

Dad touches me shoulder, opens the front door and leaves.

I hold the handle. Feels cool against me sweaty palm. Maybe Tommy was right. I should have stayed at home.

I'm afraid of what I'll find when I open it. That Mam won't want anything more to do with me. This is what Tommy must have felt like before his reading. Steeling himself for his big moment, trying to turn fear into excitement. Easier said than done.

Open the door to find Mam sitting on the sofa, her head turned towards the window. She watches as Dad trudges slowly up the street.

She turns to me. I'm shocked. For the first time ever, Mam looks old.

'Sit next to me, Ryan.'

I do as she says.

Then she does something I'm not expecting. Mam leans over and wraps her arms tight around me. I put me arms around her. And we stay like this for a long time.

Mam finally breaks free and leans back to look at me.

'So, you've got a brother.'

'Aye.'

'How does that make you feel?'

'Dunno.'

'Don't turn into your dad. Tell me the truth, Ryan.'

Not sure what the truth is anymore, as far as me feelings are concerned, but I've come all the way up here. Got to give it a go.

'Part happy. Part sad. Happy to have a brother. Sad the way it's happened. I was a bit in awe of him at first. Thought he was Mr Perfect. But realised he's got problems, same as everyone. We've had a few issues, but think we've sorted them out. I like him.'

'Good answer, Ry.'

'What about you, Mam?'

Her eyes drift off me. Her hands clench and unclench.

'Didn't think I could hate your dad anymore, but find I've still got some room to spare. Can't believe he kept that lie for all those years. How ironic. His son, his other son, is the one to unmask him. There's justice for you.'

I touch her arm.

She smiles, but in a second it's gone, like a snowflake on a barbecue.

'I had a feeling Tommy was his son.'

'Really?'

'Yeah, really.' She picks at a nail. 'Knew about the affair. He admitted that much. But assumed it was buried in the mists of time. But when we split up, he seemed desperate to get a job down in London, even though he had a good job up north. I thought, it can't be to do with that woman, can it? Thought it was all over between them. But I guess Tommy meant it could never be over. Didn't find out she had a son until just over a year ago, when I learned he'd been sent to prison. Then I found out his age. Born not long after your dad's fling. Way too much of a coincidence. Confronted your dad about it. Course he denied it. Denies everything. But the feeling never went away. Deep down I knew.'

'Why didn't you tell me?'

'Couldn't prove it. And what good would it have done?'

'Is that why you hated me moving in with him?'

'Aye, I guess it was.' She raises her eyes to meet mine. 'Once I heard you and your dad were moving in with her and Tommy, it was the final kick in the teeth. Couldn't take it. He had the perfect little family, and I, I had nothing. Didn't even have you.'

Sobs break from her.

I edge down the squeaky sofa and hug her. But the hug doesn't work. She cries even more. Mam clings to me as if I'm on a cliff edge, about to slip from her grasp. Her tears wet the shoulder of me T-shirt. I finally understand the hurt she's been feeling. The lies. The betrayal. The loss. I can't forget some of the bad things she said. But how would I have reacted if it had been me? Need to look at her not as me problem mam, but a mam who's had problems. Most of which had nothing to do with her.

At last she stops crying, dries her eyes and blows her nose on a tissue.

'Okay, pull yourself together, you silly woman.'

Sounds just like Gran.

'Dad says he didn't know Naomi was pregnant with Tommy when I was conceived.'

'He would say that wouldn't he? The perfect alibi. But I've only his word for it. And we know how much that's worth.'

'Why would he have me if he knew he already had Tommy?'

'Men do strange things, Ryan.'

I nod. Don't ever want to tell a lie that wreaks so much havoc, hurts so many lives.

It's time for the truth.

'Mam, I don't want things to go on the way they have between us.'

'What do you mean?'

'I feel like I've been bossed around.'

'I don't want to control you, Ryan.'

'Maybe that's not what you meant. But that's how it feels.'

If this has hurt Mam, she hides it well.

'My only ever concern has been your welfare, Ry. You know that.'

'I want to be able to tell you anything.'

'You can.'

Here goes.

'I've stopped me piano lessons.'

Mum looks shocked, for a split second. Before a smile takes over.

'Thought *The Sound of Music* sounded a bit crap.'

We both laugh.

'Ryan, if that's what you want, then so be it.'

Thought Mum would go mad. Shows how little I know.

'Anything else you want to get off your chest?'

Here goes.

'I don't want to go to America.'

Try to read her face. But can't.

'You're right, Ry. That was a stupid idea. No one's going to America. You need to stay and finish your education. I want to stay here, be near you. Even though you did send me to a wedding that didn't bloody exist.'

And she gives me the best smile I've seen in a long time.

'You've got your whole life ahead of you, and a brand new brother.' She squeezes me hand tight and smiles. 'Crazy how I've only seen this Tommy once. He's probably not a bad lad.'

Never thought I'd hear Mam say that.

'And you helped Tommy to read.'

'Aye. Tried me best.'

'Course you know your dad's dyslexic.'

'What?'

'Aye, when we first met his reading and writing were terrible. But we found a specialist, like we did for you.'

Can't believe that in a house with four people, three of us are dyslexic.

'So Tommy and I both get our dyslexia from him?'

'Aye, probably.'

So much to take in.

'Your dad spent years away from Tommy, missing all his big moments. I don't intend to do that. Even living here, I realise how much I miss you. I want to get a flat closer to you. I want to be there for you. I love you, Ry. I love you so much.'

Teh raeding

We move into our house, but apart from a new address not a lot's changed. The atmosphere has followed us. Things have calmed down, but reckon it's going to take a helluva long time for things to get back to normal. Don't say much at home, apart from to Ryan. This lack of talking has meant I spend a lot more time reading, thanks to my new dyslexia specialist, Mrs Carlton. She's a lot better than Ryan. Won't tell him that. Already learned to touch type, and my reading and writing are getting so much better. Go through about a book a week, and if the story's a good one, I can totally forget about those two downstairs, and what they did.

Then I got a message. Just a few words, but enough to drag me from my bed. I put my coat on and walk up the street, trying to think what to say. But I put the thinking to one side. Wasn't me who sent the message. They can do the talking.

I enter the park. Spot a can on the grass. Tempted to give it a kick, but the can stays un-booted. She's on the same swing as last time. The one I was on, the day Ryan found me. I sit next to her, rocking back and forward, gently.

'Hi, Sprout.'

'Hi, Dish.'

She looks different.

'New haircut?'

'Not that new.'

Haven't seen her since that day at the café. Take a long look at her. There's nothing about her I don't like. Apart from her feelings for me.

'Thanks for the card.'

'Cool. Happy birthday, Alice.' Even though it was ages ago.

She stares off across the park at some guys throwing a rugby ball.

'I heard about your family.'

'How d'ya hear?'

'WhatsApp.'

Silicon Valley was built for moments like this.

'How you feeling, Tommy?'

Grip the chains of the swing. 'Crap.'

'Can imagine.'

No, you can't. What with your sweet mum, and a dad who was there at your birth, and the birth of your sister Chloe, and brother Noel. A family built on love, instead of mine. Built on lies.

'How are things now?'

'Stalemate. Our house is like a warzone. Without the bullets.'

Alice smiles.

We set our swings moving.

'You've got a new brother.'

'Yeah. When you get a new sibling you imagine them being brought home from the hospital in a basket, chubby face, tiny toes and fingers. You don't expect a ready-made, fully grown teenager.'

Funny to think the only good thing to come out of this is Ryan, Piano Man.

'He even helped me with my wedding reading.'

'What do you need help for?'

'Cos I'm dyslexic.' Alice's mouth drops open. 'Ryan found out his dad's dyslexic too. Runs in families. So the guy not only ignores me for seventeen years, he gave me dyslexia.'

'But the card you wrote was perfect.'

'That's because I didn't write it. I mean, the thoughts were mine, but the spelling, punctuation. That was Ryan.'

'What you gonna do about it?'

'I'm seeing a specialist. Getting it sorted.'

We sit there for a while, gently rocking.

'Why did you text me?'

'Wanted to see you.'

'Well, here I am.'

But it's the person who's not here that's preying on my mind.

'How's the new boyfriend?'

Alice looks down at her scuffed trainers. And then at me.

'He doesn't exist.'

'What?'

'I made him up. Needed to create some space between us. Shouldn't have said it. But it just came out. I'm sorry, Dish.'

Feel both good and bad. Good that she's not seeing anyone, bad that she had to lie to me in order to get away.

'Why didn't you say you didn't want to see me anymore?'

Alice breathes in.

'Because that would have been a lie too.'

My smile grows bigger as the realisation of what she's said hits home.

'Maybe we could do this again,' she says.

'What? Sit on the swings and listen to me droning on about my pathetic parents.'

Alice kicks my foot again. 'No, stupid. Meet up and talk… about something else.'

She looks off, smiling. 'Didn't know how much you meant to me, Dish. I thought I'd got over you. I tried to get over you. But failed miserably.'

'What about *your* parents?'

'What about them?'

'Do they know you're seeing me?'

'Mum does.'

'What did she say?'

'Be careful.'

'What does she think I'm gonna do?'

'Mum reads a lot of thrillers. She's got a vivid imagination.'

We laugh.

'I'm glad you texted me, Sprout.'

'I'm glad too.'

She reaches over. Her hand touches mine. And stays touching. It's the first time anyone has done that since the wedding. Alice has no idea how good it makes me feel.

'Shame you weren't at the wedding.'

'Yeah,' she says, squeezing my hand tight. 'I'd have liked that. No, I'd have loved that. Bet you looked good. Got any pictures?'

Didn't take a single selfie the whole day. Couldn't bring myself to do it.

'Sorry.'

'It's okay.'

'But I can give you one of the highlights.'

'What do you mean?'

'My reading from the wedding.'

Alice's eyes light up. 'You've got it with you?'

'Don't need to. It's all up here,' I say, tapping the side of my head. Been through it so many times reckon I could have done it from memory on the day. But didn't want to take the risk. Instead I relied on Ryan's extra-large words.

'Oh, do it for me, Dish, please.'

'Sure you wanna hear it?'

'A million per cent.'

She releases my fingers, allowing me to compose myself. May only have an audience of one, but I feel every bit as nervous as I did in the church.

Alice leans forward on her swing and closes her eyes.

Just breathe, Tommy. Just breathe.

I look out across the fields and begin to speak.

'How do I love thee? Let me count the ways.
I love thee to the depth and breadth and height
My soul can reach, when feeling out of sight
For the ends of Being and ideal Grace.
I love thee to the level of every day's
Most quiet need, by sun and candlelight.
I love thee freely, as men strive for Right;
I love thee purely, as they turn from Praise.
I love with a passion put to use
In my old griefs, and with my childhood's faith.
I love thee with a love I seemed to lose
With my lost saints,—I love thee with the breath,
Smiles, tears, of all my life!—and, if God choose,
I shall but love thee better after death.'

Phew.

Never thought I'd have to deliver those lines again.

Look over and see Alice staring at me. Tears have pooled in her eyes.

'Oh, my God, Tommy, that's so beautiful.'

'I didn't write it.'

She laughs.

'Stand up.'

I do.

Alice gets off her swing, walks over and wraps her arms around me, and holds me tight, like Mum did the day I got out.

'I love you, Tommy Cavendish.'

Rseult's Dya

Peel off the foil, take the little plastic lens from the container and ease it on to me eyeball. The world goes from soft to sharp in the blink of an eye. The world's greatest invention may be the wheel, but in second place is definitely the contact lens. How can a tiny circle of silicone and plastic bring everything into focus, change your face and boost your confidence all in one go? No idea, but it does.

Check me reflection. Chin is as smooth as ironed sleeves. Me shaving has got so much better.

'Hurry up, Ryan, man, we're gonna be late.'

Dash into me room, looking for me best shoes. That's the problem with having a bigger bedroom, more room to lose things. Me second best shoes will have to do. Put them on and hurry downstairs. They're waiting in the hall, Dad, Naomi, Tommy and Alice.

'Here comes flyin' Ryan,' says Tommy, as I jump the last few steps to the ground.

'Come on, let's go,' says Dad.

We climb into the car, Naomi and Dad in the front, me, Alice and Tommy in the back. Can feel the warmth of Alice's thigh pressed next to mine. Tommy will be feeling the benefit of her other thigh. He's lucky to have someone as gorgeous as her in his life. Hope I meet a girl like her one day.

'You all right in the back?' shouts Naomi.

Two 'yeahs' and one 'aye.'

And for once no one is lying. Things are all right. The war that raged after the wedding was followed by the odd skirmish, until everyone grew so sick and tired of fighting that peace broke out. I think Alice played a part. A big part. Tommy finally got his girlfriend back. And his confidence wasn't far behind. A happier Tommy made for a happier house.

After a short journey we pull into the pub car park. Although me stomach's never seen the inside of a gym, whatever muscles live there begin to tighten. *The Magpies.* The same place we went the day Tommy got out. Feel guilty about the stupid thoughts I was having back then. So much has changed. We're all different to the people who were here before.

Dad parks up and we go inside. It's a lot busier than the last time. But then today is a special day.

A waitress shows us to our table and hands us the giant menus.

'Would you like me to take your drinks order?' she asks.

'Yeah, let's have a bottle of your best champagne and five glasses,' says Dad.

It's not a soft drinks sort of day.

The waitress returns with the bottle and glasses, opens it with a muffled *pop* and pours the drink. We each take a glass.

'Well, I'd like to raise a toast,' says Naomi, 'to our two very bright lads, sorry, young men. To Ryan and Tommy.'

'Ryan and Tommy,' say Naomi and Dad and Alice.

We clink and drink.

It's GCSE results day.

I got five nines, four eights and a seven. Tommy got three eights, three sevens, and three sixes.

We're both happy with our marks.

Tommy's dyslexia specialist really helped. Like to think I played a small part too. Although I was never really up to the job, hope I gave him the boost he needed.

Dad clinks a spoon against the side of his glass.

'And an extra piece of good news. Seeing as you've both worked so hard, Naomi and I have agreed to waive the money you owe us for last year's incident.'

Tommy and I fist-bump each other. Then Dad and Naomi. Getting the money was proving a real pain. I haven't found a summer job yet, but managed to sell some old clothes online. I reckon so far I've earned enough to pay for a wing mirror.

'Got something else to celebrate,' says Tommy. 'My post-release supervision comes to an end next week.'

'So you can now do what you want?' says Alice, excitedly.

'Yeah, rob banks, steal cars, anything.'

'Tommy. Not funny.'

'Sorry, Mum.'

He buries his head in the menu.

Dad comes to his rescue. 'What are the specials, Tommy?'

He picks up the piece of paper from the table and reads. 'Salmon and spinach with tartare cream. Truffle chicken and potato gratin. Roast cauliflower with caper dressing.'

Word perfect.

'Yum,' says Naomi.

Can't help but think of the person not at the table.

Mam.

She finally moved out of Gran and Grandad's, and found a new flat and a new job in London. Like Tommy it's taken her a while to get over what happened, but every time I see her, she's a little bit brighter, a little bit better. Mam's found a group of women to play tennis with. But said she's not looking for a mixed-doubles partner. She was over the moon at me results and to celebrate said she wants to take me away somewhere for autumn half-term. I'd like that. Maybe a place you won't get jet-lag. Like Cornwall.

'Everything okay?' says Naomi, who's spotted my expression doesn't match the occasion.

'Aye.'

Everything really is okay.

Teh prsenet

'Hi, Mum.'

'Oh, hi, Tommy.'

She's in the middle of making their bed.

'Want me to help?'

'Sure.'

We grab the sheet and float it down on to the mattress.

'How much on your side?' she asks.

'Nearly on the floor.'

She pulls it until it's even. Can't let Mark have more sheet than her. We tuck it in, and then do the same with the top-sheet.

'Where's Ry?'

'In the pool.'

They haven't won the Lottery. The pool is three metres across and made of plastic, but big enough for four people to wallow in when the sun's out.

We put the duvet on, flatten it, tuck it in, and add the pillows. Mum and Mark each have a pillow to sleep on, plus five others, in ever decreasing sizes, which serve no purpose at all.

'Why have you got all these?'

'Pillows are like shoes. You can never have too many.'

You say so, Mum.

I stand up straight and take a deep breath.

'Ur, I've got something for you.'

Mum looks confused as I pull a tiny package from my pocket and hand it to her. She tears it open to reveal a small bottle of her favourite eau de cologne. Wasn't cheap. That's the thing with perfume. The smaller the bottle the more expensive it seems to be.

'Oh, Tommy, that's lovely.'

She hugs me. And doesn't let go.

It's only a bottle of perfume.

But I guess it's more than that. It's a sign I've finally forgiven her for what she did. I'd promised to never hurt Mum again but hadn't bargained on her hurting me. We'd both done things we'd wished would stay hidden, but they'd been uncovered, and come back to punish us. Time has gradually chiselled away at my anger. I realised she's the same Mum after the lie, as before. The silence has been replaced by words. And words by actions. Like this.

We hold each other until she breaks away and kisses me on the cheek.

'You're a good man, Tommy.'

A question.

'Your new name's Cavendish-Dyer. Does that mean I have to be called Tommy Cavendish-Dyer?'

'No, you keep your name.'

What I wanted to hear.

'You should go join Ry, before I make a complete fool of myself,' she says, looking lovingly at the little bottle.

Go to my room, change into my swimming shorts and head outside, via the fridge. Grab a couple of lagers and walk to the garden where I find Ryan lazing in the pool, baseball cap on, shades on.

I step in. The water is beyond freezing, but I keep this to myself. Got my image to think of. Ease myself in next to Ryan, and hand him a bottle.

'Refreshments for Mr Dyer.'

'Thanks.'

Only a few more days until we start school again. My A-level subjects are physical education, art and English. Would never have added English a year ago. But it's there now. Thanks, Mrs Carlton. Thanks, Ryan.

Let the sun go to work on me. For the first time in a very long time I feel good. Take a swig of lager and look around. So glad we moved. No longer have to face that garage I climbed down from, the fence I jumped over, and the back gate I was frog-marched through by the oversized officer. Instead I've got a whole load of different bricks and fences to look at. Ones that mean absolutely nothing.

The same goes for the neighbours. No idea if they know what I did, but if they do, they don't show it. Which suits me fine.

Then there's the guy who was so desperate to meet me.

'Got a text from Logan Williams,' I say, resting the cold bottle on my chest.

'Who's he?'

'The leader of the gang that got me locked up.'

'Damn,' says Ryan, looking at me over the top of his sunglasses as he rises from the water. 'What's he after?'

'Wants to meet up. For a reunion.'

'What did you say?'

'"Sorry, Logan, bit complicated, I said. My girlfriend's dad is a detective inspector." Last I heard from him.'

Alice's dad and I have never got on, but he's come to my rescue in a way he could never have dreamed of. Finally got Logan Williams out of my life.

'Result,' says Ryan, as he slips back into the pool.

Take another drink and turn to him.

'I wanna say thanks, Ry.'

'What for?'

'For accepting me. And for helping me when you didn't have to. I know at times I've been a total idiot. But then so have you. Must run in the family. The idiot brothers.'

Ryan smiles and clinks my bottle. 'The idiot brothers.'

I lie back against the edge of the pool, basking in the moment.

From the kitchen door appears Mark in his running gear. He's wreathed in sweat. 'Looks good in there,' he says, wiping his brow.

'Yeah, water's warm. You should come and join us.'

'Not falling for that, Tommy. Looks like you two could do with more supplies.'

Even though we don't, I'm not about to argue.

He disappears into the house and returns with two lagers. Hands one to Ryan.

'Cheers, Dad.'

Hands the other to me.

I've struggled with words all my life, and one word in particular, but it's here now, patiently waiting its turn, like a customer in a long queue. I've never said it before. Not to the person who it belongs to. Maybe it's time.

'Thanks, Dad.'

He smiles and walks back into the house.

I look up at the sky. Blue fills my vision. It's going to be a good day.

The story behind the story

Words are the oxygen on which a story lives and breathes. While finding the right ones can be hard, I've never struggled to see them, or put them down on the page. But I've come to realise that for many, the act of reading or writing is neither simple nor straightforward. This was brought home to me when I was asked to write a short film about dyslexia, and the effects it has on a young boy and his family. The film is called *Mical,* and tells the true story of Pat and Mike Jones, who went on to develop the amazing dyslexia learning tools known as Nessy.

Having been inspired by Pat and Mike, I decided to write my own dyslexia story, exploring the impact the learning difficulty can have on young people and those around them. I didn't have to look too far for sources of inspiration. My teenage daughter Tallulah has dyslexia, as does her cousin, Amber. The more I searched, the more I discovered how common it is. As many as one in five people have dyslexia, and while most are given the support they need, many go undiagnosed. This became the catalyst for *Read Between the Lies,* the story of a teenager whose efforts to read lead him to a discovery that could destroy his family.

Malcolm Duffy
Surrey
March 2022

Acknowledgements

Finding the right words is no easy task. It not only takes time. It takes people. I'd like to thank some of those who've helped me find the words to tell this story and understand what it means to have dyslexia.

A huge thanks to: Mike and Pat Jones, Tiffany James, and all the people at Nessy, for their insights and help in understanding the issues around dyslexia. Caroline Bateman for her wise words and advice. Tallulah and Amber for helping me understand what it means to be dyslexic. Sinead MacCann, at the Howard League for Penal Reform, for her insights into the world of juvenile offenders.

And for reading between my lines an enormous thanks to: my agent Davinia Andrew-Lynch, editor and publisher Fiona Kennedy, Lauren Atherton, Megan Pickford, Sophie Wills, cover designer John Gray, and everyone at Head of Zeus.

Me Mam. Me Dad. Me.

- Winner of Sheffield Children's Book Award 2019, YA Category
- Winner of Redbridge Children's Book Award 2019
- Shortlisted for Waterstones Children's Book Prize 2019
- Shortlisted for Waterstones Children's Book Prize 2019
- Shortlisted for Bristol Teen Book Award 2019
- Shortlisted for Southern Schools Book Award 2019
- World Book Night title 2019
- Nominated for CILIP Carnegie Medal 2019
- Longlisted for Branford Boase Award 2019

Sofa Surfer

- Shortlisted for Redbridge Children's Book Award 2021
- Nominated for CILIP Carnegie Medal 2021
- Longlisted for UKLA Book Awards 2021
- Children's Books Ireland Free to be Me Reading Guide 2021
- Selected for Empathy Lab Collection 2022

Useful organisations

British Dyslexia Association

If you have any issues regarding dyslexia, visit the British Dyslexia Association website at bdadyslexia.org.uk or call 0333 405 4555.

Nessy

Nessy is the world's most popular website for dyslexia information. To learn more about their award-winning programs go to nessy.com

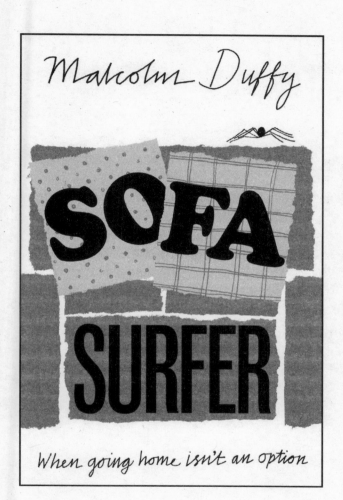

One

You never forget the day you lose your home.

I lost mine on a Tuesday.

I'd been doing maths homework. Evaluating exponents. Torture.

'Tyler,' shouted Mum.

'What?' I grunted, more to me than her.

'Tyler,' she cried again.

Guess it must be dinner. Or I've left a shoe lying around somewhere. Not bothered, really. Anything that stops maths is good to me. I closed my books, went downstairs, and looked in the dining room. Nobody there. No knives or forks or placemats out. Must be something else.

'We're in here.'

I dragged myself into the sitting room. As soon as I set foot inside I knew something wasn't right. For a start, Mum and Dad were sitting, squidged tight together on the sofa, holding hands and smiling: something they only do when they've been drinking. What made it stranger was that they didn't seem relaxed. They were perched right on the edge, as if there was something exciting on TV, which there wasn't. It was Sky News, with the sound off.

'Sit down,' said Dad.

I flopped on to a chair. Tallulah, my little sister, was already sitting cross-legged on the floor. The air was crackling with anticipation. For the first time ever I realised that the gold clock on the mantelpiece made a ticking sound.

'What's happened?'

'It's not what's happened. It's what will happen,' said Mum, squeezing Dad's hand, as they looked at each other with faces still debating whether to be happy or sad.

'We're going to move,' said Dad. From his voice, from his expression, from his body language, from everything, I got the impression I wasn't going to like what came next.

'Up north,' said Mum.

The oxygen level in the room dropped as Tallulah and I took in two extra-large portions of breath.

'Up north?' said Tallulah.

Mum and Dad nodded in unison.

The clock on the mantelpiece could not have ticked any louder.

'Why?' I asked.

'I've been offered a job in Bradford.'

'Where's that?' said Tallulah.

'Yorkshire.'

'Where's that?' said Tallulah.

They clearly weren't big on geography in Year Four.

'It's a big county. Up past Gran and Grandad's house.'

I stared at the TV. The presenter looked as if they were in a fish tank, mouthing silent words. I half-expected a banner to appear along the bottom: *Breaking news: the Jackson family to leave London.* I'd once got hit smack in the face by a ball in the playground. My parents' announcement was comparable to this.

Tick. Tock.

Over the last few months I'd heard them talking about properties and job opportunities and stuff like that. But that's all I thought it was – talk. Didn't for one second think the talk would actually turn into anything meaningful, like action. Mum and Dad aren't exactly the intrepid type. Dad's an accountant. His big love is golf, which is also his big hate, judging by the look on his face when he comes back. Mum works in HR, which I think is where you deal with people who hate their jobs. So why did they have to go and be vaguely adventurous?

'Well, say something,' said Mum.

But it's hard to find words when your brain's out of order.

I finally found one, hiding in a corner.

'When?'

Mum took a big breath. 'Your dad starts work in three months. I'm going to find a new job. In the meantime we'll start searching for a new home.'

Tick. Tock.

'But we've got a home.'

Mum and Dad swapped looks, as if to say, *Who's going to take this one?* Mum stepped up to the plate.

'Tyler, your dad's been given a great opportunity. We're both really stressed out working in London. It'll be a new start for all of us. Also, the air quality here's not getting any better. It'll do my asthma the world of good to get out of town. And we'll be nearer Gran and Grandad in Derby.'

She'd obviously been working on that list.

'And then there's the crime,' she continued.

'What crime?'

'It's all around us. A boy got stabbed in Richmond last week.'

'Three stops away on the tube. Big deal.'

'It was a pretty big deal for his parents.'

Mum gets worked up about stuff like that. Even cries at the news sometimes.

'Where will we live?' said Tallulah.

'We'll find somewhere nice,' said Mum, smiling at Dad for support. 'Maybe a village somewhere.'

'A village?' I spat, with as much disgust as I could muster.

'Or a small town.'

'I don't want to go.'

'Lots of families move.'

'Lots of families stay put. I want to stay here.'

Dad looked at Mum, as if to say, *Told you he'd be a nightmare.*

'You've got to give it a chance.'

But I didn't want to give Yorkshire a chance. I didn't want to give anywhere a chance. I wanted to stay here. Where I live. I'd heard enough. Got to my feet and stomped towards the door.

'Tyler,' exclaimed Mum. 'We haven't finished.'

But I had.

Went upstairs as noisily as I could, kicked open the door to my room, swept all my maths books off my desk and fell backwards on to my bed. How could they do this to me? I've got everything I want here. Everything. My squad: Ben, Asher, Tom, Lucas, Reggie, Mason. Brentford FC, a bus ride away. A school I don't hate anywhere near enough to want to leave. And last but not least, I've got London, the city with a squillion things to do. The place everyone wants to move to. So what do we do? Leave it for some crumbling village, up north.

I put my hand against the wall. I don't think it's possible to love a wall, but I loved this one, and the three I couldn't quite reach, and the bedroom door, and the floor and the windows and the ceiling. It wasn't the greatest house in the world, but I suddenly realised how much it meant to me. It was part of my life. A picture popped up in my mind. Me in the hall, in a Moses basket, one day old. It's the only home I've ever known.

I took my hand off the wall and put it to my face. The cool felt good. My face was burning. Didn't think I could get emotional over a house, but that's what their news had done to me. Tears began to escape. They didn't want to go to Yorkshire either. They wanted to stay here, where they belonged. But I knew deep down it wasn't going to happen. I'd seen the looks on Mum and Dad's faces. They'd made their minds up. We were leaving.

Two

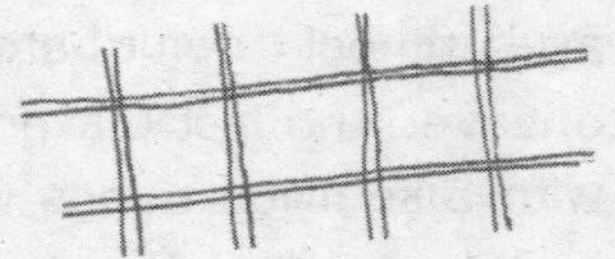

Fast-forward six months.

I now live in Ilkley, West Yorkshire.

And I hate it.

Our new house has all the usual stuff – front door, windows, drainpipes, roof, rooms. It's also got something else, a stupid name – *Fairview*. Maybe it had a fair view once, when it was built by the Victorians or whoever. Now it's got a view of a road and three lock-up garages. But Mum and Dad love it. Or they seem to love it. Don't really care. All I know is that my home is over three hundred kilometres from where it should be.

Our house isn't the only thing screwing up my life. It also happens to be the start of the summer holidays. What's wrong with that? This is what's wrong with that: I'm faced with weeks and weeks of nothingness, trapped in a place where excitement has been abolished, with no mates whatsoever. Well, not entirely true. I have made two friends, Dom Kingham and Jack Goddard, but right now they may as well be enemies. Dom's gone to his parents' house in France for the entire summer, and while Jack's still here, he might as well not be. The only thing I can rely on him for is being unreliable. We arrange to meet. He cancels. We fix up a game online. He's busy. I think while he's number one on my new friend list, I'm at the bottom of his. I only get a look-in when his other mates are busy. Probably in his contacts as *TLR: Tyler, Last Resort.*

I miss my old home like mad.

Might sound a bit odd, but I took photos of all the rooms before we left, and every now and then, I lie on my bed and look at them on my phone, remembering everything that went on there. The kitchen window I broke with a football. The sitting room, where I found my badly wrapped bike one Christmas morning. My bedroom, where I used to hang out for hours with my mates, my real mates. The downstairs cupboard, where I used to throw my school jacket. The bathroom with the toilet I puked in when I got gastroenteritis.

I didn't tell Mum and Dad about the photos. They'd only go mad.

Tyler, you've got to move on.

Where to?

Thought I might have got over it by now. But I haven't. Even though the rooms are familiar, I still hate them, like kids in class you can't get on with, no matter how hard you try. It's as though our old house has died and I'm the only one who's sad.

Mum's got a new job. Always said she wanted to work

from home, and now she does, as a content moderator for some social media company. Has to watch all that horrible stuff online she won't let me watch, then tell someone to take it down. From the look on her face by tea time, she's more stressed than she ever was in London. Not that she'd ever admit it.

Dad's also got a new job and works really long hours. The country doesn't seem to have done much to relax him, and he turns into Mr Moody when he gets home. At weekends, he goes walking after a golf ball with some neighbours.

The family member who's most in love with Ilkley is Tallulah. She seems to have made friends with just about every single seven-year-old in town, and her summer comprises a diary full of play dates. Good for you, little sis.

But Mum was right about one thing. In half a year of living in West Yorkshire none of us has been stabbed.

There was something else good to come out of moving up here.

Dexter.

When we moved, Mum and Dad promised we could get a dog. As bribes go, it was champion, as Yorkshire people say. I've even put him in the contact list on my phone, with a made-up number. Loneliness does weird things to you.

Time for one of his walks.

In the kitchen, there he is, ever-ready Dexter, tail wagging, eyes wide open, tongue unfolded, waiting to go. It's all you have to do to make a dog happy. Open a door. Dexter's a Border Collie. Farmers often use them as sheep dogs. Not that we have any sheep. The only thing he has to herd is me.

I grabbed his lead from a hook on the wall and walk outside.

'Bye, Fairspew.'

We went down the street, and across the fields towards the River Wharfe, me at a trot, Dexter as if he'd been shot from a canon. We reached a big wooden gate, but before I could open it, Dexter was already on the other side, squeezing flat on his belly and squirming through, desperate to reach the open space. We crossed Riverside Gardens, Dexter darting this way and that, but never far from my feet, as if attached by an invisible string.

'You love it here, don't you?'

Dexter's tongue flopped out. Dog speak for, *Yes, you idiot.*

Fields and woods and hills and lakes and streams. Perfect if you have four legs. Not so perfect if you have two. And you're fifteen. And friendless. And bored.

'Want to chase sticks?'

That's the most stupid thing you've ever said, Tyler.

I found a big stick and threw it as far as I could. Within seconds it was back at my feet, covered in slobber, ready to be launched again.

'Wonder what my friends in Chiswick are doing now?'

Dexter looked at me. Clueless.

I used to FaceTime them, but not any more. Just too painful. Seeing them, but not being able to be with them. Hearing about the things they'd done, reminding me of all the things I hadn't done. Mum says we can go and visit them some time, but that would be torture too. A few hours, when what I'm really after is weeks. And then heading back up the M1. In slow-moving traffic.

'I still hate them for what they've done. What do you think of my parents, Dex?'

Dexter squatted and did a poo.

I laughed.

Briefly.

I'd forgotten the poo bags.

I looked around to see if anyone had spotted Dexter's curly calling card. Luckily there was no one near, and I hurried away. Probably get arrested here for doing something like that.

We crossed the bridge over the River Wharfe and past the rugby club.

'Can you believe we're not even going on holiday this year?'

Dexter seemed happy at this news. No kennels for him.

'How could they choose a new kitchen over two weeks in Spain?'

Unable to answer, Dexter ran off.

Typical. The one year I most wanted to get away, we stay put. Mum had her heart set on an island with a granite top, twin sinks, and cupboards. I had my heart set on a different sort of island. Mum won.

What was I going to do? While I loved Dexter, I couldn't walk him every minute of every day. His paws would be down to stumps by September. I needed to find something else to fill my days. Something that didn't cost much. Something that maybe gave me the chance to meet someone. The answer came a few minutes later.

As we turned into Denton Road, I saw a white building in the distance, surrounded by a wall. A place where many hours could be happily killed.

Ilkley Lido and Pool.

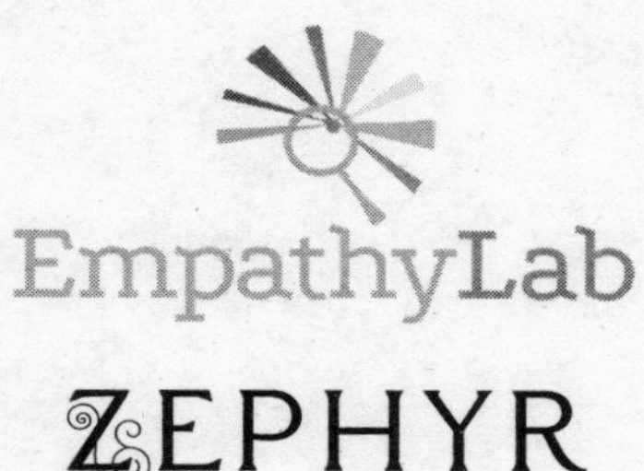

We are an Empathy Builder Publisher

- Empathy is our ability to understand and share someone else's feelings
- It builds stronger, kinder communities
- It's a crucial life skill that can be learned

We are supporting **EmpathyLab** in their work to develop a book-based empathy movement in a drive to reach one million children a year and more.

Find out more at www.empathylab.uk
www.empathylab.uk/what-is-empathy-day

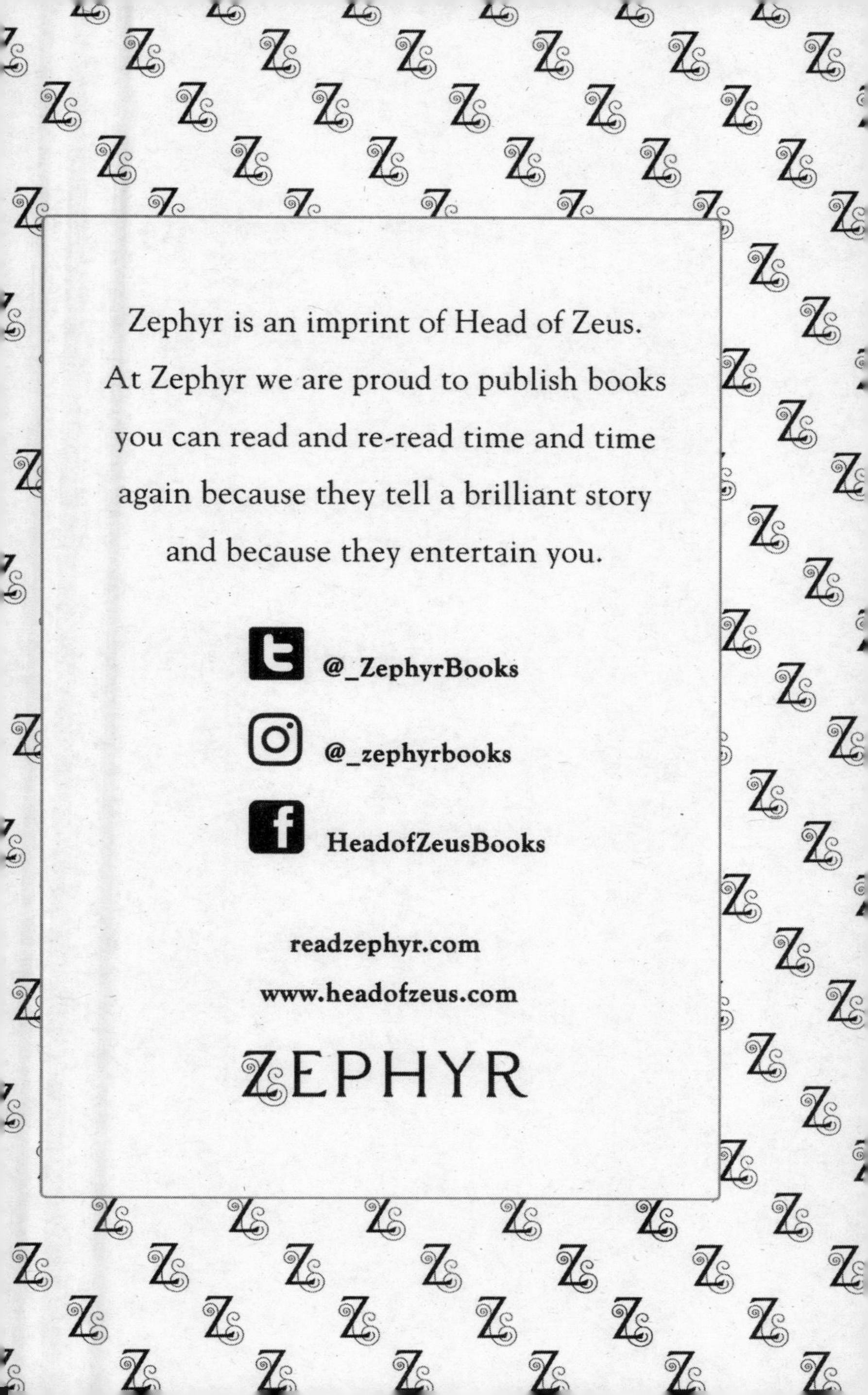
Zephyr is an imprint of Head of Zeus.
At Zephyr we are proud to publish books you can read and re-read time and time again because they tell a brilliant story and because they entertain you.
@_ZephyrBooks
@_zephyrbooks
HeadofZeusBooks
readzephyr.com
www.headofzeus.com
ZEPHYR